GW00375114

Spell me a Witch

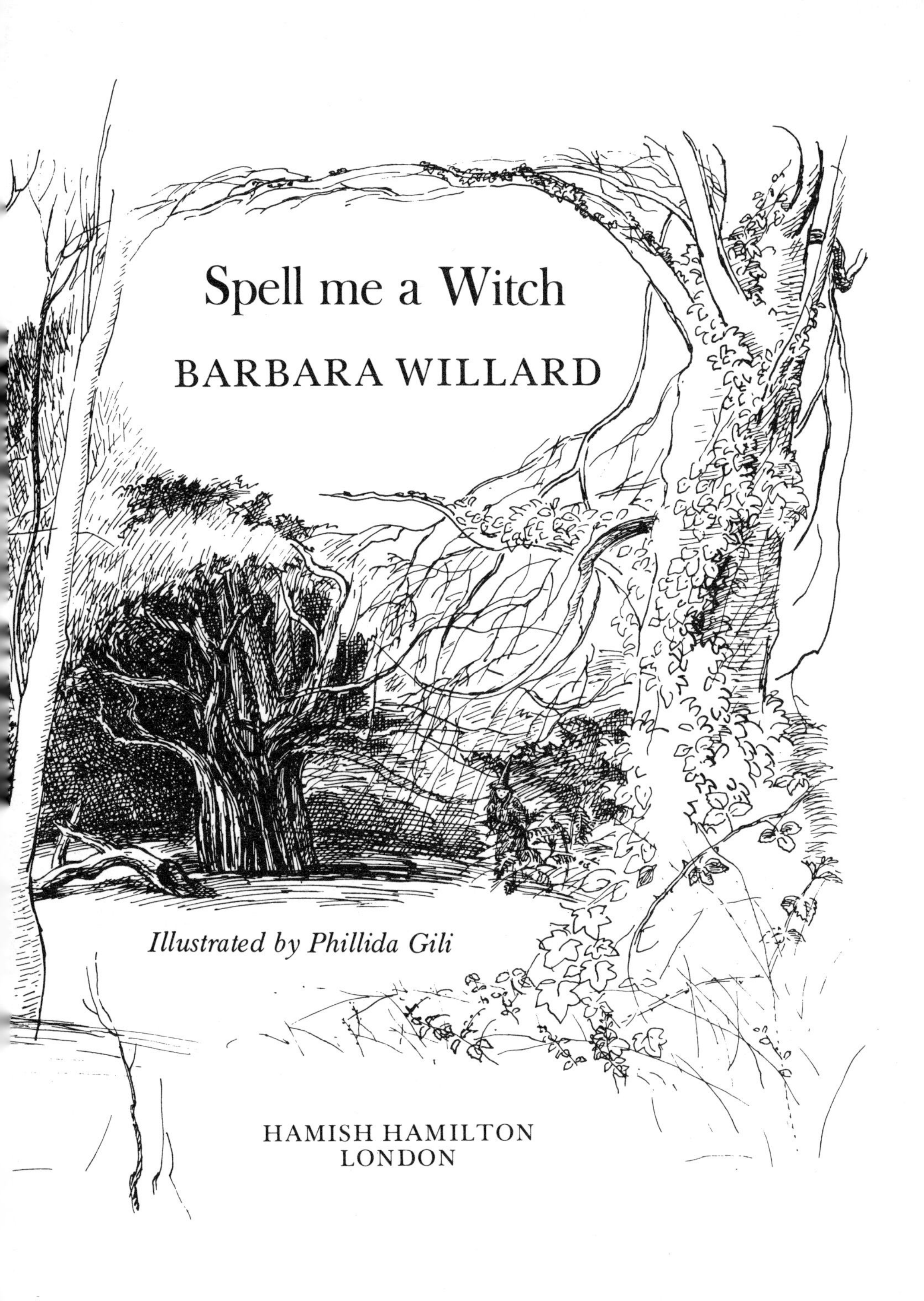

Spell me a Witch

BARBARA WILLARD

Illustrated by Phillida Gili

HAMISH HAMILTON
LONDON

First published in Great Britain 1979
by Hamish Hamilton Children's Books,
Garden House, 57–59 Long Acre, London WC2E 9JZ

Reprinted 1982

ISBN 0 241 10084 4

Filmset by Pioneer

Printed and Bound in Great Britain by
Redwood Burn Limited
Trowbridge, Wiltshire

For Belladonna
The Betonies
and
All the little Witches

Contents

1. *Something Terrible...*

The pupils – there were nine of them – stood on the wide steps at the door of The Tower, waving to their Principal as she set out on her journey. At last she was entirely out of sight and their hands grew still, their arms dropped to their sides. A gleam came into their eyes, however.

"Three days!" cried the wickedest of them all, mistakenly named Angelica. "Three whole days she'll be away at the stupid old Conference! Just think what we can do in the time!"

"And just think what we'd better not do," said one of the older but less clever ones.

"You can do what you like! I'm going to enjoy myself!" cried the wickedest. "And I think, just for a start, I shall turn you all into pale pink mice!"

The youngest squeaked as if she was a mouse already.

And certainly all sorts of extraordinary things had happened before now to the pupils at The Tower.....

Before the final meeting was properly over, Belladonna Agrimony slipped quietly from the Conference hall and made her way to the cloakroom to collect her broomstick. All she wanted now was to get home to her girls as soon as possible. This was less because she missed them and longed to see them again, than because she could not trust the little wretches not to get up to some ridiculous exploit while her back was turned. Betony, her assistant, her second-in-command or whatever one liked to call her, should be able to control the pupils, of course. Her trouble was that in spite of her rigorous training she had somehow never learnt to be tough.

Belladonna was quite exhausted by the Conference, which had kept the highest order of witches, the Sevenly Sisterhood, behind tightly closed doors for three long days. She yawned as she crossed the wide hall, with its beautiful sweeping staircase. The Sisters always chose stately homes for their autumn meetings – all but a few of these were safely closed to the public by Hallowe'en. They were nice and quiet and neglected – a bit scruffy, perhaps, after all the tramping visitors, but who cared about a few cobwebs and spiders? Certainly not the ladies of the Sevenly Sisterhood.

Belladonna went into the cloakroom – and there was her least favourite sister, Euphorbia, seated before a mirror, brushing out her elf-locks. Hearing the door open, Euphorbia instantly switched off her reflection; then, seeing who had come in, gave a light cackle and flicked it on again.

"Force of habit," she explained. "Silly me! I've been working in some rather tight corners lately. So I'm slightly jumpy."

Belladonna was accustomed to Euphorbia's boastful ways. She grabbed her broomstick and made at once for the door.

"I really must fly!" she said.

"Oh I did hope we might have a nice witchy little gossip," said Euphorbia, neatly back-combing her last lock and smiling so that her gaps showed. "How are all your girls? How is dear Betony?"

"Much as usual," replied Belladonna. A faint twinge of the memory made her shiver slightly. What might they be up to, she wondered, precisely *now*?

Euphorbia's mean green eyes were flashing with malicious fun.

"So lovely for you to be able to leave them with absolute confidence!"

"Lovely," agreed Belladonna, now more than halfway through the door. "See you next Equinox, I daresay."

With that she slammed the door and went fast across the great hall to the imposing entrance, with its carved marble figures holding aloft torches. Drawing her big cloak around her, Belladonna Agrimony paused a second to get her bearings. Again that curious twinge. Shaking off a sensation of foreboding – most uncomfortable – she mounted and rode away.

(And what *were* they up to, back at The Tower, while Belladonna was busy about her own concerns?

"Oh *no*! You can't, Angelica! You simply mustn't!" one of them was crying.

"I mustn't – but I shall!"

"Stop her, someone! I don't believe she knows all the words! It's a very complicated spell!"

"I know enough," said wicked Angelica. "Stand back, everybody!")

Few things can be pleasanter than riding a reliable broomstick through a moony autumn night. It is best of all when home is at the end of the journey, as it was for Belladonna. She lived in Sussex, some few miles south of East Grinstead, where a sizeable forest offered everything needed for the practice of her craft. . . Everything? Perhaps that was too bold a claim. Change had hit Belladonna's chosen profession as it had hit many another. Solitude was so important, and although her Academy for Young Witches stood on the ideal spot, once outside its boundary the pupils were likely to be subjected to all sorts of pressures and distractions.

For although the number of witches in the world has remained more or less steady for centuries, the number of people, plain, ordinary people, has gone up by leaps and bounds. They have to go somewhere. It was annoying for Belladonna that at weekends and during the holidays the forest was where a great many of them could be found. There had already been one or two tiresome encounters.

First, a young pupil, not yet proficient in even Simple Invisibility, had found herself face to face with a party of picnickers (or *pink-knickers* as they were naughtily called by the pupils). Instead of just quietly turning away and making for home, the child had panicked. She had run across the picnic spread so nicely on the ground, kicking over tea and orange juice and trampling through a large chocolate cake. It had *Happy Birthday* written on it in pink icing, which made matters even worse. The very word *happy* should cause a sharp, piercing pain even to a child-witch at the beginning of her training. . .

The second occasion that Belladonna recalled with a grinding of the teeth, concerned a pupil named Diantha. A young man, each morning of one spell of fine June weather, had parked his motor-bike near the pond, and gone off on foot into the deeper places of the forest. He was hunting rare plants – but what he bagged was a most unusual girlfriend. . . Belladonna and her pupils tried to charm Diantha back on Midsummer Eve – a delightful, old-fashioned ceremony – but nothing came of it.

("Oh *Angelica*! *Now* look what you've done!"
"Mop it up, silly," Angelica snapped.
"It'll be all right in a minute," someone said hopefully.
"I don't think it will! Oh! Oh! Look!"
"Fetch some more buckets," said Angelica. . .)

The night was wonderfully clear. By the time she had crossed the Thames and was above Croydon, Belladonna could see as far as the downs. She gained altitude and then, far and silvery, she saw the sea – at that point on the coast where a narrow river draws bright curves along its valley.

"The forest is still a perfect situation for the Academy," she said to herself. "Even as things are, it could be a century before anyone realises the place is where it is."

At one time she would have had her cat to talk to, but Musina had grown old and been retired. She had not been replaced, but that was all part of life's changing pattern; few of the sisterhood ran to a trained cat nowadays.

And now Belladonna saw her forest spreading ahead over gentle slopes and mounds, the heights crowned with clumps of trees, or caps of gorse, or mantles of heather. She lost height and came smoothly beaming in. She pulled out a neat little walkie-talkie and gave her call sign clearly and quietly:

"Necromancer One. Necromancer One to Sorcerer Two. Are you receiving me? Over."

Instantly she heard the switch, and a split second later Betony's well-known voice reached her — but over a most extraordinary hubbub. Youthful voices shrieked and squeaked. There was a clatter and a huge gushing sound that Belladonna hardly dared interpret. Surely they had not been tampering with *that* hoary old spell?

"Mistress, mistress!" came Betony's agitated cry. "Is it really you? Something terrible has happened! Come home! Come home! Something terrible has happened! Something terrible is *still* happening! Are you receiving me? Something terrib. . . ."

Belladonna had cut out without replying. She began to descend much faster — a good thing she was wearing her spring-heeled boots, for the landing might be, at the very least, sudden.

Ahead of her now she could see The Tower, rising up out of its huge sheltering circle of mighty magic yew trees, themselves encircled by an outer ring of protective hollies. The Tower stood gaunt and forbidding in the moonlight – the place where, for years unnumbered, she had conducted with enormous success her Academy for Young Witches. . .

Now, as she came to it, she was aware that the building was bulging and creaking with activity. Even at her present height she could hear shrieks, screams – frantic, even hysterical.

The moonlight, white as hawthorn blossom, showed up every detail of The Tower's beautiful surroundings, setting black bars across the landscape, turning the sheets of water to unblemished silver. . .

Sheets of water. . ? Unblemished silver. . ? Belladonna had surely never looked grimmer than she looked now. She should have known better than to leave them for so long, the silly little witches! Now she was close enough to see that at every window, every door, small figures appeared and reappeared with buckets which they emptied at frantic speed. The Tower had the appearance of some huge and elaborate fountain, the sort of thing featured in the pleasure gardens of Giants. .

She saw at once what had happened. She had left instructions for The Tower to be cleaned from top to bottom while she was away. Like many other apprentices in magic, they had tried to employ the Bucket-and-Water spell to halve their labours, magicking their broomsticks to carry the buckets for them. And like many before them, they had obviously let the spell get out of hand. They had set the buckets and brooms in motion but they had no idea how to stop them. . . It was all so elementary; they had been taught already about not tampering with even a really old-fashioned spell like this one.

Belladonna made a perfect landing, and instantly Betony was at her side. Her hat was wobbling on the back of her head, her hair was in wild wet ratstails. She looked desperate.

"It was Angelica, mistress!"

"Of course."

"Well, then," said Betony, helplessly. "Oh please do *do* something! I've tried and tried – but I just can't spell it out."

Belladonna allowed her gaze to travel slowly from window to window from which the water wildly cascaded.

"The exercise will do them all good."

"They're *exhausted*, mistress. It's been going on for *hours*!"

"Of course it's been going on for hours!" Belladonna shouted. "You should know, and so should they all, that the Bucket-and-Water spell *does* go on for hours. That's the whole point of it. Lucifer send me patience! This is Lesson One in *The Magic Manual*. The merest baby of a witch is taught about it, and that it is *not to be tampered with*! Are you going to tell me that you have forgotten the precept?"

"Oh dear," murmured Betony. "Something about *when water runs* – sorry, *when water flows*."

"*When water flows by magic, magic three-and-thrice alone may quell it.*"

"Your magic is ten-and-tenth, mistress. So please, please!"

"My magic, Betony, is one-thousand-and-thousand."

"Yes, of course. I just meant that even if it were only – Oh dear – I don't think I know quite what I do mean."

Belladonna gave Betony a sharp look. No one else in all her long life had been such a worry to her. She had always been able to see straight through everyone. But with Betony it was different. How it was different she was unable to fathom – an anxiety in itself. As she thought of this and the strangeness of it, a dreadful doubt assailed her. It was not altogether a new doubt, but she had never known it so powerful. Suppose – only suppose – she could not reverse the spell her little sillies had set in motion? Suppose she was to be the very first qualified witch to be defeated by this absolutely classic enchantment?

A cold and clammy hand seemed to touch Belladonna's scalp. Her hair prickled almost to the point of throwing off sparks. She drew a deep, deep breath, opening her mouth, hoping that if she just rushed at the business the right words would come tumbling out.

"Acqua mista, acqua plana! Acqua resista, catasta! Extante! Exulto! Exculpo!" She had been whispering hoarsely, but now the whisper rose to a frightful shriek. "Fin! Finto – finto! Fintessimo. . . *Nemo more*! Cessit!"

The last word was hissed out, and with dramatic, almost alarming suddenness, the water gave a kind of gulp, spurted for a second, then with a huge, slirruping noise, as if it were being sucked back into The Tower, the flow faltered, thinned, trickled, died.

"Caldate brumo in bruma," concluded Belladonna.

There came from inside The Tower a great clattering as the buckets were hurled aside, and many small voices joined in a cry that was half sob, half song. Then from the main door of The Tower the little witches, Belladonna's pupils of whom she hoped so much, came tottering in raggedy exhaustion, falling over one another, tumbling and rolling down the steps from the terrace, all skinny arms and legs, with hair on end and dirty faces, with hats askew or altogether missing, with dripping clothes which, as they collapsed on the grass which had instantly dried, dried too. They were too weary even to realise that the Principal stood there, gazing relentlessly at the heaps and mounds of child-witch, only waiting her moment to flay them with her fury. . .

"They are punished enough," Betony murmured in her ear.

"I am to decide! Tell them to stand up! Call them to attention!"

"Might it be later?" Betony urged. "Send them to their beds now. They can go without supper, if you like. Speak to them in the morning."

"*I* shall decide. It is for me – for me to say what shall be done!"

Yet on the very point of shouting out some harsh command, she paused. She was feeling pretty tired herself. The Conference. . . the flight home. . . the effort of cancelling the Bucket-and-Water spell had been altogether greater than she cared to admit. Her bones ached. But her pride ached more. Yes, indeed, she had pulled it off, and every section of the disenchantment had worked perfectly. But at what a cost. Nothing could cancel out the bitter fact that she had all but bungled it, that she had *doubted.* She, Belladonna Agrimony, with nineteen M-levels, a double-first in Necromancy, with her Harridan's License unblemished and a degree in Invisibility from the University of Thin Air, had been uncertain of her own powers.

Such a faltering must come as a terrible shock to any witch. To one as distinguished as Belladonna it came like the threat of thunderbolts. She needed to be alone. She must consider her situation. Was this the beginning of the end for the Academy of Young Witches? What next. . . what next. . ?

"Send them to their dormitory, Betony," she said in a hoarse, faltering voice. "I have to consider what's worst to be done."

She turned, tripped over her broomstick, and was actually thankful for Betony's swift grab at her elbow.

"Let me help you to your room, mistress," murmured Betony, soft and solicitous.

Belladonna thrust her away.

"To Hades! Who are you to talk of helping me?"

Betony stepped back modestly, bowing slightly as Belladonna passed her and went indoors.

Up and up the stairway that spiralled all the way through The Tower to Belladonna's own room that was called Tower Top, too weary even to magic a wafting that could save her old bones. As she went, the witch all but echoed Betony's words, her cry over the little radio: *Something terrible has happened*!

Alas – Belladonna greatly feared it had.

2. *Betony and the Others*

To understand the rather curious relationship between Belladonna and Betony it is necessary to go back a bit — and even then the matter is unlikely to become altogether clear. Impossible, too, to say precisely how far to go back, for a highly qualified witch quickly moves out of the area of common time. Our days, weeks, years are as nothing and no witch ever stops to consider how old she is. Certainly Belladonna had been around for simply ages.

"I began at the Palace," she would sometimes say.

She had taken over the Academy for Young Witches from her Aunt Digitalis who, one Midsummer Eve, melted into thin air. The Academy in those days had been for a long while very comfortably established in the ruins of the Old Palace, situated on high ground to the north west. Belladonna herself had been educated in witchery there, starting in her very early childhood – which was why she claimed to have begun "at the Palace".

The Old Palace was said to be haunted, which meant that no one went near it. Gradually the ruins had crumbled right away. Brambles and birch scrub had grown up and covered everything that was left. People sometimes say, even now, "There was once a great Palace where Kings stayed when they came to hunt the deer through the forest." But nobody knows exactly where such a place can have been.

The present quarters of the Academy, The Tower, had originally stood on the outskirts of the nearby market town. A very complicated Transportation Spell had been operated to move it to its new site. It had taken some time, beginning on May Day and coming to completion the following Hallowe'en. It had been moved 'image by image' as described in *The Magic Manual* (Chapter Seven, pages 19 to 74.), and then re-assembled on the chosen spot. So, of The Tower, also, you might at that time have heard people say, "There used to be a tower, a water-tower, I suppose, standing near those new houses they built last year. . ." It had gone so gradually no one had noticed what was happening, and though in this case people remembered where it had been, no one could recall when the building disappeared, or why.

Or where it had gone. . .

That, of course, was the important part. For now it stood amid the ancient yew trees and their defending ring of holly – and these spoke of an older magic than that practised by Belladonna Agrimony and the Sevenly Sisterhood. A strange power – hanging in time like some discarded satellite in space – rayed out from the great ring of trees and kept intruders at bay. . .

Any moment now we shall get to Betony. But perhaps the little witches – pupils, students, trainees, call them what you like – had better be dealt with first. Who were these children?

It is well known that there are no married witches. There are married ladies who think vaguely that magic might be useful in many ways – but they are always much too busy to do anything about it. It is their unmarried sisters who take up the craft – or if they do not take it up themselves they usually see to it that some promising niece is quietly encouraged to take instruction. These children have to come from fairly large families, where the disappearance of the odd one is not so likely to be noticed. No very great supply is needed, since, once they are qualified, witches last for such ages. At the time we are concerned with, Belladonna's establishment, along with one other in Scotland, run by a trio of rather weird sisters, could easily turn out all that were required.

Nine or ten pupils filled up The Tower very adequately; nine were at this time in residence; a propitious number in affairs of magic.

And now, at last, to Betony: —

Pupils were mostly found abandoned by their plotting aunts and wandering near The Tower. They often took some time to stop crying for home, settle down and decide that Magic is Fun. Betony came to The Tower in a very different manner. She was discovered by Belladonna herself, so extremely young that she had been simply wrapped up in old newspapers and dumped on the front doorstep.

"What in the name of Lucifer am I supposed to do about this?" Belladonna had demanded of Potentilla, a prize pupil of that time who had stayed on to serve her apprenticeship.

"A baby, ma'am! It's a baby!"

"I can see that perfectly well for myself. But what happens next?"

"I should throw it away at once! Best not to waste time in such cases. Let me spell a disappearance for you — I am well able to."

"I'm not entirely convinced of that," Belladonna said. "We don't want one of those half-a results. I've seen some pretty funny ones in my time."

She was holding the parcel of baby and peering into it

with distaste and puzzlement, when the creature opened one eye. The eye was a startling, marsh-gentian blue and it stared up at Belladonna, absurd as it seems, in a distinctly challenging and defiant fashion.

"My goodness," muttered Belladonna. "I mean – my badness!"

The eye closed. The mawkin's face crumpled. It began to cry.

"Ugh!" cried Potentilla, covering her slightly pointed ears and shuddering. "What a revolting noise! Do throw the thing away, ma'am!"

For a second or two Belladonna was thoughtfully silent, while the baby bawled and hiccupped.

"I think I'll keep it," she said at last. She added rather hastily, "It might come in useful."

"*Useful?*"

"Well – you know what I mean. . . There's many a spell – of an advanced order – that calls for such specialised ingredients as very small children can supply. Milk teeth, for example. Tears. . . Go quickly, Potentilla, and fetch me a little flask – a little crystal flask. It's a pity to waste the material we have here now. Infants' tears keep well. I'd be a fool to miss the chance of harvesting a few."

Off went Potentilla, glad to be out of earshot. Belladonna sat down on the step, with the strange wailing parcel on her knee. She gave it a sort of bounce, then said something — then looked anxiously, guiltily round to be sure there was no one about who could have overheard. For "There, there!" she had said, in a thoroughly un-witchly voice.

Potentilla was back in no time with the flask, and Belladonna was able to get it half-filled and securely stoppered before the baby, in obvious surprise at these goings-on, abruptly stopped crying. . .

Those tears Belladonna had never had occasion to use. The crystal flask, with its sapphire stopper, still stood among other phials of rare ingredients in her small private dispensary. The fluid had gradually condensed and become a heap of tiny pearls at the bottom of the flask.

And just as her tears had become pearls, so the baby had become Betony, a creature of some beauty, dark, slim and devoted – an excellent, an almost perfect personal assistant for any witch of distinction and high standards.

What was it, then, that made Belladonna frequently uneasy about Betony – even, dare it be said, a little scared? In her darkest and most dismal moments, in her most secret of secret thoughts, Belladonna knew what it was and did not attempt to pretend otherwise. At such times, wringing her hands or tearing at her locks, she knew beyond doubt that Betony was a reflection of herself – her better self, that she had defeated when she was no more than a slip of a normal girl (dark and slim) just introduced, somewhat slyly, to the charms and diversions of magic.

When the little witches maddened their teacher, Betony would say, "They didn't mean it." "They won't do it again," she would promise. "Give them another chance." And even, "It wasn't really their fault." And when Betony said such things, that quality in her that was poison to Belladonna's peace of mind always won the day. Belladonna *did* give them another chance, she almost believed they would not do it again, she accepted that it wasn't their fault.

Quite simply, Belladonna's witchiness was declining.

Though she had scoffed when Euphorbia spoke mockingly of 'retirement', such a thing might become a distinct possibility if her weakness could not be overcome.

A few days after the business of the Bucket-and-Water Spell, three of the little witches were out on the forest gathering materials for love potions. Such preparations might seem unsuitable in positive witchcraft, more the sort of thing to be obtained from Wise Women or even the Health Food Stores. But the love potions that Belladonna's pupils learnt how to prepare were a different sort altogether – they were extremely powerful as well as being malicious and expressly intended to get people most appallingly mixed-up. Once brewed, they were ranged on high shelves in locked cupboards. To be honest, they were not much used, though the Sevenly Sisterhood had the right to demand supplies if they needed them.

The three little witches busily employed in searching out various important herbs, were Angelica, Tansy and Borage. Tansy was extremely young and inexperienced, but so promising that she was nearly always with the older two. Borage was clever, too, much more inclined to nastiness than anyone now at the Academy. Angelica was also wicked, but in a less serious and much more amusing way. If there was ever any particular mischief in the making, then the idea would almost certainly have come from Angelica – as in the recent matter of Bucket-and-Water.

So now she said thoughtfully to the other two, "I wonder what sort of potion we might make if we mixed pennywort with crushed allium?"

"A nasty potion," said Tansy.

"A potion of writhes," said Borage; and smiled at the thought of it.

Tansy asked, "What's writhes, Angelica?"

"Oh – anyone knows what writhes are. Don't they, Borage?"

"Well – *I* know."

"A snake with a stomach ache is writhes," announced Angelica.

Borage laughed rudely. "It's a good deal more than just snakes, my dear. I read in a book about allium and pennywort. A wicked princess mixed it for her lover. He writhed and died."

"Who could we try it on?" Angelica wondered dreamily. (No wonder Belladonna had often said that Hogweed or Spiderwort might suit this pupil better than Angelica as her magic name.)

The three of them sat down thoughtfully. The bracken had just this week changed from autumn gold to autumn red, and when the little witches were seated, the fronds waved well above their heads. Even though they were not bothering about invisibility, they were entirely hidden.

"Have we actually got any pennywort?" Borage asked.

They all picked over their gatherings and found plenty of both ingredients. The allium, of course, would need extracting and properly distilling, and the pennywort must be dried and then powdered. It all began to seem a bit too much like hard work. Someone would smell the allium if they worked on it in the distillery by themselves; and suddenly Borage began to wonder if what they really wanted was not pennywort but pennyroyal. They had picked none of that and the nearest they could think of was miles away.

"We must just stick to the old love potions after all," Borage decided. "What's more, we'll have to get on with the job. Didn't Belladonna say they must be all mixed and ready by dawn? A Messenger's coming for them."

"Goodness! Help! That means the night shift!" cried Angelica. "It's ages since we had a rush job. Oh, *really*! Sometimes I wish I was just a dear little girl at boarding-school."

A cry of wild derision broke from Borage, a giggle from Tansy.

"Imagine Angelica in a blazer!"

"She'd have to write essays!"

"And make her bed properly every morning — no good trying to magic boarding-school blankets!"

Borage and Tansy laughed with increasing wildness and rudeness, flinging themselves back in the tall bracken and spluttering helplessly.

"I should have a nice neat gym slip, my dears," said Angelica primly, "and two lovely long plaits."

"Pigtails!"

"All right – pigtails."

"Hockey! Girls at boarding-school play hockey! They'd make you play!"

"Then I should win," snapped Angelica.

"You couldn't take your magic with you!"

"Why not? I bet I could! I've a good mind to try it – just to show you!"

She shouted it out. Immediately, the other two were still and silent. Then Borage spoke, bringing the words out slowly and carefully, as if she were proud of them.

"I – dare – you!"

Angelica blinked. She was sitting upright, cross-legged and neat. Her face set into a scowl and she glared at Borage.

"Done!"

Tansy began to look anxious, even frightened. "W–when?" she asked, no more than whispering.

"Never mind when. You'll know when, won't you, because," said Angelica, rising gracefully without putting her hands on the ground, "I just shan't be there. Shall I?"

Tansy jumped up in her turn and ran round Angelica helplessly, wringing her hands, crying, "Oh no, Angelica! Don't! Suppose something went wrong? Borage didn't really mean it!"

"Didn't I just," said Borage, leaning on one elbow, nibbling at a piece of fungus she had just found growing nearby.

"But what if you're not clever enough, Angelica?"

"I'm very clever, Tansy."

"You'll need to be," said Borage, narrowing her eyes and looking just about as unpleasant as any witch of her tender years could hope to look.

"Oh dear!" Tansy cried. "Oh Betony – quick! Where are you? Help! May Day!"

Angelica clapped her hands over Tansy's mouth before she could make the call that could easily summon Betony to the spot. "Be silent, you silly brat! There's only one thing to do with a dare – and that's accept it. If anything goes wrong – then it'll be Borage's fault!"

With that she flung Tansy back among the bracken, made an evil sign at Borage, and stalked off. The tall bracken stirred and waved behind her. She was gone. When – oh when – would they see her again?

About half an hour later, as it happened – and even after that, two whole days and nights passed without anything unusual taking place. Certainly Angelica was in a very funny frame of mind, not answering when she was spoken to, staring into the distance, biting her nails. The Academy pupils were encouraged to wear their nails long in preparation for the time when, as fully qualified witches, they would wear talons. It did seem as though Angelica could not quite work out the spell she planned to cast – and how could she be expected to; clever as she was, she was also very young and inexperienced.

"I think she's changed her mind, Borage," Tansy said. "Do you think she's changed her mind?"

"I don't think about her at all," Borage answered, with a magnificent sneer. She was easily the most accomplished sneerer of them all and had won the annual award in this subject two years running.

Then it was the third day after Borage's challenge to Angelica. It was dinner time. They always sat down to table promptly at noon, in the old way.

A very pleasant thing about the Academy was the excellence of its food. The most delicious dishes were magicked daily by Old Hemp, the semi-retired Crone who looked after the kitchen and the catering arrangements. She was so withered, and so leathery, and so hairy that it was a chestnutty old joke to say that she was really a wizard. It was actually Betony in one of her light-hearted moods who had nicknamed Old Hemp "the Wizard of Nosh".

At some time during each morning, probably not so long after dawn, Old Hemp would proceed out of the kitchen and survey the forest beyond the encircling yew and holly. She might spot a tender young deer standing prettily against a leafy background, or a neat little pig strayed from a nearby farm in search of acorns. Old Hemp had only to work her magic, and wonderful venison pies, succulent pork chops, delicious deer-and-pig sausage appeared on the table.

That third day after Angelica had made her rather silly remark about wanting to be a dear little girl at boarding school, there was a most mouth-watering dish of tender pork set down on the dinner table. Angelica had as good an appetite as the next witch, and she was savouring the perfect flavour, mouthful by mouthful, and looking dreamily into the distance – when suddenly her eyes snapped back as if they were on elastic and a very thoughtful gleam appeared in them.

Nobody but Angelica herself knew that the spell she had been working out, in a laborious and junior way, had at that moment moved a step nearer to its completion – indeed it might be the very final step that had been suggested by one of the ingredients on the dinner table. . . .

"She's up to something," said Borage to herself; few things escaped her and her witchly future was pretty well certain to be a successful one. She kicked Tansy under the table and Tansy very stupidly yelped – then bit her lip as Belladonna frowned and peered at her.

"Be silent, Tansy! You must listen."

For they always sat silent at dinner while Betony read aloud from some enchanting book. It might be *The Sorcerer's Calendar; A Black Thought for Every Day of the Year,* or the very popular and funny *Spell-It-Again*; or perhaps a poem from that collection called *Witching Hours*, which was said to contain some work by the great Merlin himself.

This reading was one of Betony's duties as Personal Assistant to Belladonna. It meant that she had to hurry over her own meal and finish in half the time allowed to the rest. She had a magic digestion but she always looked a bit undernourished.

Betony cleared her throat after the interruption and began again. She chose the poem called simply *Dragon.* A shiver of anticipation ran round the table, for this was a favourite – they were sure that this, of all the poems the book contained, could only be the work of mighty Merlin. None of them ever noticed how Belladonna smirked behind her hand, for she knew better – in fact, she had written the poem herself at a quite different period of her long career.

"Get on with it," she commanded Betony now, snarling to conceal her malicious amusement.

So Betony read:

" 'Talons ten to the Dragon,
Ten, ten, no more;
Fire singing in his belly
By ancient lore;
Fire burning on his breathing
By magic rite;
Power, power to those pinions
That know no flight. . .

Cent bright scales to his quarters,
Fork his slim tail;
Lavish his lair with lichen
And nightshade trail. . .
Nothing known of the Dragon
Save what I tell –
Yet these words once spoken
Ring around Hell. . . .' "

Always when Betony finished reading, one of the pupils had to take over – Belladonna liked to pounce on one of them without warning, pointing and crying in a dreadful voice, "You!"

So, today, looking round the table and seeing Angelica so much taken up with her own curious thoughts, Belladonna snapped out, "You!"

Angelica did not answer.

"Angelica!"

She stirred and looked round. "Mmmm?"

Betony thrust the book along to her.

"Page one thousand and two. Do wake up, you silly little witch."

But Angelica put the book aside, and rose from her place, and without a word to any one of them, or so much as a glance, she walked slowly and thoughtfully from the room, swinging the door behind her.

"Bring her back!" commanded Belladonna Agrimony in a terrible voice.

Two or three of them, enjoying the commotion, ran to the door and tugged at the handle. They tugged and tugged. The door would not budge. Minutes went by, while Belladonna sat irritably tapping the table with a pepper pot, and turning almost black and green with rage.

"Have you forgotten *everything* I've taught you? Are you incapable of the simplest exercise? Cannot you even magic an obstinate door?"

They tugged and they tugged, muttering and whispering, more and more joining in – first Chervil, then Tarragon, then Caraway and Spurge, until only Borage remained at the table. But they were all so flustered by Belladonna's awful manner and appearance that their poor little minds were completely emptied of all common sense.

"Betony!" roared Belladonna at last. "Open the door!"

Still seated at the table, lazily and gracefully Betony waved her left hand, describing a certain figure on the air, and murmuring as she did so,

"Ovento. Oventa. Portnabulis oventibus."

The door then flew open, knocking the lot of them backwards in a mound of nervous giggles.

"Return to your place, Angelica," commanded Belladonna in a huge voice.

Nothing happened.

The passageway beyond was empty. Empty of Angelica, too, was every room in The Tower as they ran searching and squealing, swinging up and down and round the stairs that corkscrewed from bottom to top – and, indeed, from top to bottom.

She was not there. She was nowhere at all in The Tower.

Then everyone ran outside, calling wildly, "Angelica! Angelica! Come back! Come back!"

Not a sound, not a sign. Only a squirrel chattering at the sight of them, a stoat slyly running, a hawk hovering, and one of the nearest farmer's young porkers scuttling away into the distance, squealing wildly at the noise they made and madly seeking cover. . .

"She's done it!" Borage whispered to Tansy. "I hope she knows what she's up to, that's all. She might never get back. . . ."

3. *A Few Hours to Doomsday*

Weeks had passed since Angelica's vanishment. Each day of those weeks, Belladonna Agrimony had paced moodily in her room called Tower Top, thinking, thinking – and finding no solution. Angelica, the prize pupil, had totally vanished. Where? Somehow Belladonna could not quite believe that she had vanished into thin air.

All around The Tower, the forest blazed in the last splendid days of autumn – it was so beautiful that it made Belladonna crosser than ever. She moved from window to window of her round room – there were eight of them. Once she would have been able to see with her own piercing eyes right to the farthest horizon. Nowadays she had a telescope set up in each window.

She tried them all in turn, cursing quietly at how little they showed her. Since they were fitted with lenses of spell-binding intensity they showed her everything there was to show – but not, alas, Angelica.

Almost every day, Belladonna would call up one or other of the little witches and question her closely. They had all told her everything they could think of a dozen times already, but she was certain there must be something that somebody had forgotten.

"We'll have to tell her," Tansy whispered to Borage, as she emerged for the fifteenth or so time from Tower Top. "Oh Borage – *please*!"

"I've already said – there's nothing to tell."

"Oh there is – there is! About being a dear little girl in a blazer!"

"Do you really expect me to tell her that?"

"It might help. . ."

"Help? You may be quite bright, Tansy, but you do say the most extraordinary things. Anyone can see you've got a long way to go yet. We don't *help* anyone. That's not the way to succeed in this business, my dear."

"Then I don't care what you say – *I* shall tell her! I must! I must! We've just got to get Angelica back!"

"Please yourself and you won't please me," said Borage. Flashing her eyes unpleasantly, she strolled away. . .

There has been no mention so far of Chervil in this

story. She was one of the older pupils – indeed only Betony among the young witches was her senior. Chervil had failed her finals and stayed on to take the course again. Of them all, she was the most ambitious. On her very first day at the Academy she had decided her future. 'One day,' she had promised herself, 'I shall be Principal of this establishment.' She had been quietly beavering away at the idea ever since. It had actually suited her to fail her exams and stay on. Always a bit of a loner, Chervil was a great deal smarter than any single one of the rest had ever suspected.

Perhaps it was not really so surprising that Chervil was the one who hit on the most important clue to Angelica's disappearance.

While the rest of them had run in and out and up and down, Chervil had gone quietly to the kitchen to find Old Hemp. After all, she was the one person in The Tower who had not been mewed up in the dining-room behind an obstinate door.

Chervil found Old Hemp muttering and mumbling because she had mislaid the tail and insides of the porker on which they had just dined.

"I kep' 'em for Musina," she groused. "There's little Musina loves better'n finely minced pig's innards. And the little gristly bits off of the tail fairly delights her. Look at her now. She's wild."

Nobody at The Tower cared much for Belladonna's

old cat whose days were mostly passed by the kitchen stove. So Chervil gave a rather nasty laugh at the idea of her being cheated of the innards and the gristly bits.

"We are not amewsed," said the cat primly, bringing out the only joke she knew – and what an old one.

But Chervil was already following up a startling idea and could not be bothered just then with Musina's attempts at wit. Give *innards* their grander name and they became *entrails.* The merest beginner in sorcery can hardly fail to know the importance of this ingredient in Advanced Spelling.

"I suppose you gave them to Angelica," she said casually.

"Gave 'em? I never gave 'em no one. There's nothing Musina likes better'n –"

"Yes, yes, yes – so you said... You mean she just took them without asking?"

"I never see that happen."

Musina began delicately washing one paw – the one with a white glove.

"I see that – I mean, I saw that," she said.

Chervil's whole manner changed. She flung herself down on the hearth and stroked and stroked Musina.

"Oh tell me – tell me what you saw, beautiful puss! I'll give you cream for a whole year! I'll magic you sprats for breakfast."

Musina did not reply. There was a faint, superior

smile on her wise old face and her whiskers quivered slightly.

"Tell me!" cried Chervil, her voice sharpening.

Musina rose, stretched – up with her shoulders, then out with her hind legs, a long, long stretch. She paused to flick some speck of dust from her right ear, then moved away and vanished.

Chervil stamped in fury. "Monstrous feline!"

"She used 'em all up," said Old Hemp.

"What are you talking about, you old Hag?"

"Words. She only get twelve to a day. She used 'em."

At which Chervil had rushed from the kitchen and joined the rest as they stood at last gazing helplessly over the forest. . .

For nights and nights Chervil lay wakeful, trying and trying to find some solution to the mystery of Angelica's disappearance and the disappearance of the little pig's entrails. She had tried to persuade Musina to speak again, but as Old Hemp put it, she was a miser with words and would sometimes save up her daily allowance for as long as a fortnight – or at least until she had something to say that was worth saying.

Then, after a particularly tossing night, a memory came to Chervil. It was of standing with all the rest outside The Tower and gazing searchingly over the forest, and seeing only a squirrel, a stoat, a hawk – and a small pig scuttling off into the distance.

"Got it!"

Chervil slept at last.

"Will you speak to Tansy, ma'am?" asked Betony. "She says she knows something about Angelica."

"Tansy? *Tansy*? Certainly she's the most promising of my present pupils – but she has barely a term's experience. What can she know? And anyway why didn't she say so long ago?"

"You did suggest exploring every avenue, ma'am. . ."

"Oh – oh very well. But let's be quick about it."

Betony flicked the switch of the inter-com and Belladonna moved her shoulders irritably. Every little thing maddened her at the moment. It had always annoyed her – though never so much as now – that she had not, in all the long year, contrived to work out a means of communication that needed no artificial aid.

"Tansy," said Betony, quiet and whispery into the microphone, "report to the Principal in Tower Top. Now."

Before even fast-moving Tansy could run up the corkscrew stairs, Chervil, who had spelled herself a swifter means of locomotion (top secret) arrived at Belladonna's door.

"I know!" she cried in a dramatic voice, as she stood on the threshold.

Unfortunately, a breathless Tansy scuttled in after

her and the effect was quite spoilt.

"Wait by the door, Chervil," the Principal snapped, her voice colder than ice. "Tansy — come over here."

Tansy was nervous. She had worried and worried all this time, and she was worried now, because of Borage. There were many unpleasant small revenges that could be magicked even by beginners, and Borage was very far from a beginner. So the moment the poor child opened her mouth she burst into tears.

Belladonna muttered something. Betony glanced at her quickly. But the Principal had brushed those words away — whatever they might have been — and now said, very sharply, "If you can't speak, you can go. No! Wait!" she ordered, as Tansy, helpless with misery, turned for the door. "I'll hear what Chervil has to say. I don't expect it to be much, so mop yourself up as fast as you can." She glared at Chervil. "Now — what do you want?"

"I know!" cried Chervil again.

"What precisely do you know? I have *never* expected it to be much. Indeed, in all the time I have had you under instruction, you have given little evidence of knowing anything at all."

"That's as may be!" retorted bold Chervil. "All the same, I know what happened to Angelica!"

Tansy's tears stopped as if by magic. She clasped her hands in hope and anxiety.

"Oh what? Oh *what*?"

"She turned herself into a pig."

There was a second's deadly silence. Then Belladonna snorted, and Tansy cried out she didn't, she hadn't, she couldn't, she never would. . .

"Have you a better idea, Tansy?"

"Yes, ma'am, I have. I have. It's what I wanted to tell you. Oh, I know I should have told you before, but Borage said not, and you know what Borage is. . . It was only a day or two before – before what happened. We were picking herbs for potions, and suddenly Angelica said she wished she was just a dear little girl at boarding school. And we teased her, Borage and me – only Borage was worse than me – and we said she'd have to have a blazer to wear and play hockey, and *she* said – Angelica said – she would have lovely pigtails. . ." Tansy broke off. "Oohhhh!"

"Precisely," said Chervil, smugly triumphant. "And that's what she's got. But just one. Like any other little pig."

Chervil was both surprised and delighted when the Principal, after questioning her closely and hearing all about the entrails, accepted her conclusions on Angelica.

"Well worked out – sane – useful – ingenious," were some of the things she had said. She did not, however, instantly promote Chervil, as might have been expected. The position of Betony's junior-assistant had remained empty since the departure of the last holder of the post for a more important situation. Actually, Borage was after it, and they all knew that, but Chervil did feel that in the circumstances. . . Like many another ambitious person, Chervil saw that she must somehow follow up one success with another.

So she drew herself a plan of the forest, with the little rivers marked, and the mounds and the hollows, and where the deer rested, and where the badgers played, and where each yew tree stood. Particularly she marked those strange and mysterious areas where there lurked an indescribable power that even Belladonna had never been able to explain. Then she cut her map into squares and every day she searched one or two of the squares really thoroughly. It was a big area in which to find a small pig that would answer to the name of Angelica.

It was on the tenth day, one of those last-of-autumn, first-of-winter days with a high thin sunshine, that Chervil spotted what she was looking for; Angelica!

"You don't have to worry about me," said Angelica. "I'm quite all right, you know. I have someone to look after me. I am very snug."

How strange she looked. Chervil had been quite right about the little pig part of the affair. What she had not bargained for was a little pig wearing a blazer and a round school hat, a neat white blouse and a navy blue gym slip – and conversing in what could only be called snorts and grunts.

For a moment Chervil felt almost faint. It just showed how careful one must always be when handling dangerous materials like spells. Belladonna was for ever dinning this into their heads, but this was the first actual example of trouble that Chervil had come across. There could only have been a word or two of error in Angelica's Transformation Spell – it was so nearly right, and yet so utterly, terribly wrong.

"What do you mean – snug?" she managed to ask.

"Miss Pelligrew, of course," said Angelica, spreading her trotters in a manner that suggested everything was now explained.

"Miss – Miss *who*?"

"Pelligrew. Miss Agnes Aurelia Pelligrew. She is exceedingly clever."

There is a slightly smug expression on every young pig's face, but that little self-satisfied smile they all have was in this case twice as pronounced. Angelica tossed her head and put her snout in the air while Chervil gasped and wondered. "Oh my goodness, Chervil, surely you've heard of Agnes Aurelia Pelligrew? She's quite famous."

"Who said so?"

"Well, she did, of course. She writes books, you know. Small books about small animals, and paints lovely small pictures to go inside."

"You mean – she's writing a small book *now* – about a small pig – in a blazer – and a round hat. . . With pictures of – of *you*?"

"I shall be famous, my dear! I turned up at the very best moment. I was quite worried when the spell – er – didn't quite work. But I fell on my trotters, you might say. She was wondering how on earth to find a model for the pictures. Not easy, you know, to find a pig in a blazer. Not like," she began to snort with laughter, "not like a pig in a poke!"

"I think," said Chervil slowly, "that you must have magicked yourself out of your wits. You must come home at once."

"Not likely, my dear. I'm very comfortable as I am."

"You must! You must! What you are doing is *dangerous.* What if the newspapers got hold of the story? It could mean the end of the Academy!"

"Much I care," grunted Angelica. She gave a skip or two and began to move away. "See you some time, perhaps. And if I were you – *I should mind my own business*."

Shattered by this experience, Chervil went back to the Academy knowing all too well that she ought to warn Belladonna of what was going on, of what might happen. Yet she kept silent. In her very first year at the Academy she had done well in Spiteful Intention, the most important of all lessons for intending witches. She could not easily forget that early training.

And there was another reason why she slunk home speechless. She had never before witnessed the effects of a badly bungled spell – what Belladonna called 'a half-a'. She was so shocked that she wanted nothing but to put the whole beastly business out of her mind for ever.

Meanwhile, the term was advancing. Everyone had accepted that Angelica had tried to be too clever and had turned herself into a pig, but the matter was, by order, no longer mentioned. The only change in routine was a total absence of pork from the dinner table. Old Hemp had been forbidden on pain of the direst penalties to magic any pig for the table.

All the same, they were all very much shaken by what had occurred. The Yule holidays loomed. The pupils were occupied with making enchanting Yuletide gifts – such simple spells were included as Sneezing Powder Toffies and Stink Bomb-bombs – both ideas shamelessly adapted from products available in the outside world.

Camomile – not the most promising pupil but nimble with a needle, was stitching a sampler for Betony. All the signs of the Zodiac were worked into the border, and there was a little picture of the Cinderella Spell at the point where the mice were just turning into ponies. Caraway had invented a neat pretty box with a lid that sprang open so violently it would, with luck, knock out a tooth or two; she had not yet decided who was to be the fortunate recipient.

During those last weeks of the term, too, the older pupils did Mock M-levels – but they were all in such a disturbed state of mind that nobody did well. After reading Tarragon's paper on Cauldron Care, their temperatures and so on, Belladonna really seemed likely to explode.

"The days are past," she thundered, "when young witches were imprisoned in trees for their faults. But believe me, my girl, I know how to do it – and I will do it, what's more, if you don't polish up your evil thoughts. This, for example: When lacing the brew with mice, should they be added live or dead? Answer – Let them go, they have soft whiskers! What in Hades am I supposed to make of that?"

Tarragon blushed and looked at her hands. She had been growing some quite impressive talons, but in her anxiety she had bitten them down to nothing.

At the dinner table Belladonna punished them by

changing the reading from pleasant volumes like *The Vampire's Breath* and *Mouldy Merriment* to terrible dry stuff – *Precepts of Pure Satanity*, for example, which was such heavy going they could hardly keep awake. Even Betony yawned as she read.

Things were so bad they could hardly get worse – or so it seemed. But one morning – it was snowing, and the sky was a dingy grey touched up with a sallow, bilious light that struck through the forest like jaundice – Belladonna called Betony to Tower Top; and called in such accents of despair that Betony turned pale. It took her mere seconds to materialise at Belladonna's side.

"You called, ma'am?"

"Yes, Betony. I called."

"Are you ill? How dreadfully dwindly you look!"

"That is how I feel. Dwindly and dwindled. I have received a Message."

"About Angelica?" asked Betony, eager and anxious.

"Would that it were."

"Tell me, mistress – let me share in the bad news. For I see by your looks it can only be bad."

"Bad news, as you well know, pleases every capable witch. But it needs to be bad news for others. This is bad news for us."

"Oh please! I am in the most terrible suspense!"

"The Inspection!" said Belladonna, in a voice of utter gloom.

"Oh *dear*! Already?"

"I have had it in mind – it is far more than just overdue."

"Is it really our turn?"

"Oh yes. I remember they went north last time. There was that splendid blizzard, you may recall, and two of them got blown off course."

Belladonna cheered up a bit as she remembered this occurrence. For a second or two she shook with totally silent laughter – the only kind allowed to witches. Cackles are all right, but the sound of laughter – no.

"It could happen again – couldn't it, ma'am?"

"A blizzard of such proportions? Here in the south?"

"It would be unusual but surely it could be managed?"

Belladonna looked thoughtful for a moment, but she seemed unwilling to be done out of her gloom.

"It has to be endured sooner or later. At least it will be over before Yule."

"All three of Them?" Betony asked.

"Yes, yes – they are all coming. You must see about rooms for them. Hypericum can't stand running water, remember. And Hellebore can't stand being kept waiting. In a way Henbane's the easiest. But see that you put her in a room with a north aspect."

"When, ma'am?"

"We have just a few hours to Doomsday," Belladonna replied.

4. Dreadful Preparation

Of all the Sevenly Sisterhood none were so deadly as Hypericum, Hellebore and Henbane. They were the most ancient, the most experienced, the most respected – and the most dreaded. It was not only the two Academies – Belladonna's and the one run by the three Scottish sisters – which shuddered under their piercing Inspections. They were quite likely to descend without warning on witches working quietly in secluded cottages. Some they had struck off the register for idleness and inefficiency, others they sent to work in remote areas where there was little to enchant. It had been a desperate day for the Sisterhood when these three went into partnership, and how long they had been partners it was pretty well impossible to determine. Euphorbia once told Belladonna that they had spoken quite openly of a curse they had laid on an English king who had defied them.

"They claim that he never smiled again," Euphorbia had said. "So he must have been centuries back – I remember perfectly well reading about him in my history book when I was still a schoolgirl."

The dreadful weight of all those years of malice and sorcery hung about Hypericum, Hellebore and Henbane like a great heavy cloak. Only to look at them was to tremble.

Fortunately their personal appearances were infrequent. Belladonna was not prepared to calculate how long it was since their last harrowing visit of inspection. Between jobs, if that is not too flippant a way to put it, they favoured mountain-top dwellings. Sometimes they were in Wales, driven from Snowdon by crowds and climbers, but still finding adequate lodging among the Brecon Beacons. They had given up the Cairngorms because of the winter sporters and now most often used the Grampians. Once – but that had been a mistake – they had dallied through a summer in the Cotswolds, the Influences there being very strong. Too strong, indeed.

For a time they haunted Tintagel. The tale went – and again the gossip was Euphorbia, who had had it from Penstemon, a Cornish witch – that they had clashed with a coven, or society, of local witches, mere amateurs.

"Sheer pandemonium, my dear," Euphorbia had said with glee, enjoying every second, every word of the telling. "Hellebore's hat was knocked off. Hypericum was daubed with extract of petunia – an awful colour, she still looks a bit puce, in my opinion. Henbane, for some reason, got on very well with the locals. In the end, though, she made an awful fool of herself – behaving like a TV personality, even to signing autographs."

Belladonna never quite knew whether to accept the facts of this scandalous story, much as she would like to.

"I am older than Euphorbia, and I've known them so much longer," she said to Betony, as they discussed a programme for the coming inspection. "Why – it was Hellebore who set the seal on my Harridan's License, and that was – well, it was a long time ago."

"One remembers such things, however," said Betony.

Belladonna sat back in her desk chair, uneasily gnawing the goosefeather pen she always used – a bit of an affectation, perhaps – and looked in a resentful way at Betony.

"You are so calm. Why are you not trembling at the thought of meeting these monsters of witchhood?"

"Though I am sometimes frightened, mistress, I am not on the whole very nervous."

Belladonna snorted. "We must proceed with the

programme. Where had we got to?"

"The girls to be lined up outside for a formal greeting as the Inspectors fly in. Tansy to present a bouquet of laurel and yew. Then, luncheon –"

"Remember – no pork!" Belladonna cried. "There must be no sort or species of pork eaten in this establishment till we have found Angelica. It would serve her right to be cooked – but I refuse to lend myself to such goings-on."

"Of course, ma'am."

"This is a sorry business, Betony," Belladonna said, sounding a great deal wearier than she liked.

"It is indeed. And at such a moment, too. Shall I proceed? Well, then – Singing Blackbird Pie for one course. Devilled Kidneys for another. A salad of horse-radish with curry dressing served separately. No dessert. Just green cheese and crackers."

"What are we drinking?"

"Well – if you agree. . . This is a special occasion so I thought we might broach a bottle or two of that vintage Hemlock Wine."

"Excellent. It should be pretty drinkable by now. You think of everything, Betony."

Luncheon was to be followed by speeches – a welcome speech from Belladonna, and no doubt some threatening reply from Hypericum, the strongest though not the senior member of the trio.

As usual with such visitations, there was practically no time to prepare. It was absolutely essential to scour The Tower from top to bottom and dispose of any baleful influences or lingerings of elementary magic. Such did tend to hang about because eager beginners were all too likely to employ some unsuitable ingredient – and then there was the devil to pay.

At the dinner table, Belladonna addressed her pupils. They were in a state of excitement since hearing the news, and could hardly sit still. Their Principal soon gave them instructions that stunned them utterly.

"None of you here remembers any previous inspection," she reminded them. "Such Occasions are Very Important Indeed. Everything must go precisely so. I want no slips, no fumbling, no failure to speak out. A great deal always depends on the impression made on The Three."

It should be explained that years and years ago some irreverent and waggish witch had called Hellebore, Hypericum and Henbane 'The Three H's'. This had quickly been altered by one more respectful to The Three *Ages* and then had gradually become The Three. When Belladonna announced that much depended on the impression made on The Three, she was not altogether certain what she had in mind. She had no fear of actually being closed down. But there was no denying that lately a couple of things had gone badly wrong.

Had some rumour reached the ears of the Sevenly Sisterhood? Was this so-called Inspection really an Investigation? Who were her enemies among the Sisters? Was anybody planning to unseat her and become Principal of the Academy in her place?

"We shall offer an Exhibition Of Work," Belladonna told her pupils. "Preparations will be made beforehand, all shall be ready so that there are no delays – Hellebore, particularly, cannot bear delays. You must never, never keep her waiting. Betony! Make a note. This is the rough programme."

A murmur of excitement and apprehension now ran round the table. Perhaps they were all thinking of Angelica, who could not, surely, have *meant* to turn herself into a pig – so suppose some other equally foolish and disastrous mistake should be made at this important time. They remembered, as the Principal had, and with shame, the awful Bucket-and-Water business.

"Camomile," Belladonna was saying, "you are not very clever and, I fear, are unlikely ever to become so. Therefore I shall merely appoint you attendant on The Three. It will be up to you to see that they have everything they need – and if you can't provide it you should at least be able to magic it for them – you can hardly fail to know that much."

Camomile murmured something inaudible.

"You what? Speak up!"

"I said – I should think they could magic it faster than I could."

"That is not the point. You must make a good impression. Is that clear?"

"Yes, ma'am," muttered Camomile, her teeth chattering slightly. "Thank you, ma'am."

"Then stop shivering! Borage – now that Angelica is no longer with us, you are the brightest. . . Don't dare to smile! Never employ a smile where a sneer is more expressive. Borage – you will perform Instant Invisibility followed by Immediate Materialisation. . ."

"*Instant* Invisibility? But ma'am," cried Borage, "I've only done Gradual Invisibility."

"Then you have just a few hours to learn the advanced method."

Borage sat looking pale green, and the rest of those at table tittered nervously; except Chervil, who sat stonily waiting for her name to be called.

"Tansy!"

Tansy sprang to her feet.

"You have it in you, though you are so young, to soar to the heights of witchhood." There was a slight stir, and Belladonna went on firmly, "You may think I speak too soon. But once this young witch learns to harden her heart, it is my belief she will go far. However, Tansy, you are still very inexperienced. Therefore I suggest that we leave you to do that nice little piece you learnt so quickly – The Flying Wineglass."

Tansy blushed with pleasure while the rest looked sulky.

"That leaves Spurge, Caraway, Tarragon and Marjoram. Oh yes, and Chervil. Well, five may be better than four."

They had risen one by one as their names were spoken, Chervil the last, wearing an expression of studied insolence.

"This shall be a team effort," Belladonna announced, looking from one to the other in a gloating manner. "Do you recall that exercise I taught you back in the summer – called familiarly *Now You See It, Now You Don't?*"

They all turned pale, even Chervil.

"Do you mean, ma'am," faltered Spurge, "that *table-cloth* one?"

"I do. But give it it's official name, please. What do we call it in the *Manual of Spellbinding?*"

Spurge scowled. "I can't quite remember. . ."

"*Mensa Clouta*!" cried Caraway and Tarragon with one voice.

"Correct. Kindly note that, all of you. It consists, you will remember, of removing the cloth from a fully operational dining-table, without disturbing so much as a grain of salt. Then, at the fourth count, returning it. It is the return that proves the skill of the operators. And between you, you should be able to manage pretty well." She gave a lightly fiendish chuckle. "It has to be perfect. Remember that. Perfect."

"But, ma'am," faltered Marjoram, "is it – is it *their* tablecloth we must remove? Their very one with all their food?"

"Their very one. But there are plenty of you – one to each corner as usual, but Chervil shall have the middle, though you should be able to manage without a fifth. . . Now – you may have half an hour of *Spell-it-Again* before you start work – but first finish up your delicious tabbyochre pudding."

With that Belladonna Agrimony rose, and all her pupils rose, too, to bow as she swept out of the room, followed by a somewhat subdued and worried Betony.

The moment she was gone they all slumped in their chairs again. Although the pudding was a much more delicious one than a similar sort eaten in the outside world, they all blew it away into thin air rather than do as they were told. Then they all lolled about groaning and crying out rude words and putting tiny witches' curses on Belladonna, which they knew from experience were too puny and dwindly to take effect.

"May her eyes drop out," they hissed. "May her talons curl inward – may icicles hang from her eyebrows – may – may. . ."

"What shall we do? What shall we do?" they all cried

next. "If the spells go wrong – what will happen to us?"

And four of those due to perform Mensa Clouta were almost crying – though, except for Tansy, all the pupils were presumed to have grown out of such human weaknesses.

"Well," said Borage at last, rising and stalking to the door, "I shall go and practise in the garden shed. It's about the only place where one can be alone in this ghastly establishment."

"Oh don't call it that!" cried Tansy.

"What else am I to call it? A witches' academy is meant to be ghastly, you silly little thing."

Caraway ran to Borage and caught her arm. "Hadn't you better have someone with you? We all know things can go wrong. You might need help. Suppose you do Instant Invisibility and lose the word for Immediate Materialisation?"

"Well," muttered Borage, "if I'm not back by sunset – seek me in the shed."

Spurge watched Borage's dramatic exit. She seemed less put out than the rest, though no one could tell what Chervil was thinking.

"Do stop moaning," Spurge said to the younger ones. "Surely you've got wits enough to see that if the magic goes wrong The Three are not going to blame *us*."

"No – but *she* will."

"And they'll blame her."

"Quite so," said Spurge. "Well? What's the matter now?"

No one answered. They looked uneasily away from Spurge's cold and challenging glare. Could it be – no, really, could it be that they would not like their Principal to take the blame?

"What Spurge means," said Chervil, "is that if our magic isn't strong enough, she'll switch on some of her own. Now I'm supposed to be a lot less talented than anyone else, but it is plain to me that The Three would very quickly see through that one. For my part, I shall see to it that what I attempt succeeds. And I advise the rest of you to do the same."

What Chervil did not tell them was that she planned to perform a quite different trick. She had seen Angelica again. Because of that second meeting, Chervil had got out her Abracadabra cloak that was only worn for very special occasions, and had brushed and pressed it and neatened it by tidy magic. What happened next was hidden in the mystery of the immediate future. She knew no more than anyone else whether it would work. . .

For some reason never understood, things like scrubbing and dusting, and even washing and ironing, have never yielded to magic. Window cleaning, yes; bed-making, yes; and cookery of course, being a magic in its own right. But plain housework remains obstinate, and even the ingenuity of ordinary man has never totally solved this problem. Therefore, for the last few anxious hours before the arrival of The Three, everyone in The Tower had her work cut out. The place surged and rattled like some ancient windmill in need of oiling as Belladonna's pupils set about making it spick and span.

Magic needs such cleanliness if it is to work efficiently, for even a few cobwebs can interfere with the precision of a spell. It has to be admitted that The Tower really needed these hectic ministrations. The sweeping and the mopping, the dusting and the polishing grew frenzied as it was seen how much work was required.

"No wonder I got in such a muddle the other day," Marjoram complained. "You remember, Caraway – when I gave those mice green skins. How can anyone be expected to work properly in all this mess?"

They began to mutter and grumble among themselves.

"Ought to have got at the job sooner, I suppose."

"Nobody told us to."

"Why didn't Betony say something?"

"Why should we be expected to clean the place if we're not told to?"

"I think it's disgusting."

"I've a good mind to run away."

"If you're going – I'm going."

So the grouses and grumbles went on and on, making the work seem even harder than it was. Of course they never would run away, being far gone in magic. Only Angelica would have thought herself clever enough to attempt anything so foolhardy.

At last every corner and every surface of The Tower shone in splendour. Every pupil had washed and ironed her plain apprentice's gown, mended her underwear, polished her pointy shoes and carefully brushed her hat. Between cleaning The Tower and practising their routines, few had had much sleep and they were all looking a little pale and red-eyed, but most of them were fairly hopeful that things might go well. Borage had been very successful during her session in the garden shed; she had not forgotten any necessary word and by the end of the afternoon was popping in and out of sight at such a rate that she was quite worn out.

The Mensa Clouta team had done well, too; while Tansy had executed six in a row of the prettiest little Flying Wineglasses. Camomile, in her role of personal attendant on The Three, had earned praise by setting posies of hellebore, hypericum and henbane in the three rooms – Instant Plant had always been a speciality of Belladonna's and she was delighted with Camomile's thoughtfulness.

As the last couple of hours raced away, excitement

took the place of apprehension. Half an hour before zero hour, when the little witches lined up for Belladonna to conduct her own inspection, they were all bubbling and giggling and shoving one another, knocking hats awry and behaving in a generally disordered fashion.

"Silence!"

Belladonna spoke the one word not loudly, but with a cold and slithering insistence that sent it shivering between the shoulder blades of everyone present. She was looking splendid enough to strike them with awe and respect. She wore her very high, Sisterhood hat, and her long, sweeping Harridan's cloak with the Signs of the Zodiac in copper embroidery set thickly over the shoulders. Her eyes glittered green, and she had painted her talons to match.

"Now," she said, in the absolute stillness, "let me say at once that if pleasure were permitted in our profession, then at this moment pleasure is what I should be feeling. You have all done exceedingly well. Continue in this fashion and I shall have no complaints."

Someone called out, "Mistress!"

It was Betony, stationed in Tower Top with all those telescopes to get an early sighting of The Three as they came zooming in.

"Are they coming?"

"Moving in from the north-west! Just about over

Crawley!"

"Outside, then!" Belladonna cried to her pupils. "Remember your places! Waste no time!"

Within seconds they were standing in a neat semicircle on the terrace before The Tower, Belladonna a pace or so ahead of them.

"There they are!" cried Tansy.

"Where?"

"There! There!"

She pointed eagerly with her mini-broom and all looked upward.

Far, far over the forest they saw three speeding specks. The sky was clear but as they flew a faint cloud of magic hung unmistakeably about them, the sunlight catching it and causing it to glint mysteriously. Now the specks were growing larger. They took shape. Soon it was possible to make out broomsticks, hats, cloaks billowing. . .

"There's a cat!" screeched Caraway.

"That'll be Hellebore's Walpurga," Belladonna murmured. "Hellebore is inclined to stick to the old ways. . ."

Now The Three were plainly seen. Their faces became visible, gnarled, hooked and ancient. They passed over The Tower, then swooped into reverse. In perfect formation, they flew in a spiral round The Tower, then at the last lifted to clear the heads of those assembled.

They touched down neatly at the foot of the terrace steps.

Belladonna moved at once to greet them.

5. *The Three*

The inspection by The Three of Belladonna Agrimony's Academy for Young Witches can hardly fail to pass into the history of Witchdom. This is not because of its success or its failure, but because it led on to events so extraordinary that they are bound to be recorded. It might almost be said that after its occurrence nothing will ever be quite the same in the world of witchery.

The Three, on arrival, were in mellow mood. As Belladonna advanced to meet them that day, Hellebore's cat ran flatteringly towards her and rubbed round her ankles in a manner that could only please. It seemed to be an omen, and Belladonna, who had been somewhat tensed up, noticeably relaxed.

"Thrice to all points," she murmured, bowing low.

"Thrice quick, thrice foul, and thrice to the Meridian."

She did not much enjoy being so extremely polite but manners meant much on such occasions.

"She has not forgotten the Designed Greeting, Sister," remarked Hellebore to Hypericum in an approving voice. "Many have – too many. Henbane – answer her."

"Fair is foul and foul is fair," Henbane said – then stopped. She was far and away the oldest of The Three. "I've lost the next line. . . But there, what's a couplet or two between old friends. . . You're looking pretty spry, Belladonna. More than I could say for some of our other Sisters."

"How was your flight?" Belladonna asked, ignoring the compliment for the sake of dignity, though it pleased her.

"Pretty crowded," Henbane answered her, "There's a great deal too much going on in the atmosphere these days."

"And beyond," said Hypericum.

"Oh indeed, yes," agreed Belladonna. "No escape nowadays even in the next layer."

"Still, some of these particles and fragments are rather beautiful," Hellebore said. "And one has the satisfaction of knowing that if they enter our atmosphere safely they're bound to cause a great deal of havoc."

"Are these your girls?" demanded Hypericum,

nudging Belladonna painfully with her broomstick.

"Yes, Sister. These are my girls. They are formed as a kind of guard of honour – if honour is the word. Such arrangements are always inspected, and since you have come here to inspect – start as you mean to go on, was what I thought."

"A witty notion," said Hellebore. She called to her cat. "Heel, Walpurga! Come, then, Sisters."

They moved forward together, Henbane extremely bent and using her broomstick as a prop.

"Who's this?" demanded Hellebore, standing by Tansy. Being the smallest, she was at the end of the line. "She looks very young and rather cheerful. Is that as it should be?"

"She is cheerful, not because she is cheerful, but because she is clever," Belladonna said firmly, as if that settled the matter.

"Ah. Clever. Is she?"

"Her promise is fabulous, and she is well on the way to hardening her heart. In time we shall all be proud of her."

"As you say, Sister." Hellebore moved on. "Who's this?"

"Spurge, madam," said Spurge quickly, before Belladonna was able to answer for her.

"I think I recognise a family likeness. Are you related to the Sister called Euphorbia?"

"A distant relationship, madam. It is thought she may be my great-aunt's great-aunt."

"What's she say?" demanded Henbane, poking her head forward until her old hooked nose all but brushed Spurge's cheek.

"Related to Euphorbia," Hellebore shouted. She called to Hypericum, "What d'you think? Will they do?"

"I should think exactly right. But it's early yet. That's a very accomplished sneerer you've got there," she said to Belladonna, nodding towards Borage.

"She, too, is promising," the Principal said. But she was slightly distracted by the exchange between Hellebore and Hypericum. . . Will they do? Exactly right? What was that all about?

Belladonna recalled uneasily an occasion, many decades ago, when The Three had whipped away all the most promising pupils of the Scottish Academy. They had been sent for specialist instruction to America, where there were at that time some noteable witches. Belladonna recalled a recent complaint among the Sevenly Sisterhood that there are too many amateur witches at the present time. Someone had suggested that in order to protect the good name of sorcery, these ladies should be invited to join the University of Thin Air and gain some qualifications. For such an enterprise, tutors would be needed. Of the girls at The Tower both Borage and Spurge would be likely to respond to intensive training for tutoring jobs. . . Belladonna tried to vanish the thought, knowing as well as the next witch how quickly thoughts escape, how quickly they are snapped up.

"And what of Betony?" Henbane asked sharply, breaking in on Belladonna's uneasy pondering.

"Yes, where is she?"

"Why is Betony not here?"

The Three had an unnerving way of shooting out their questions in triplicate. Belladonna replied suitably.

"She is to welcome you indoors, Sisters."

By now she felt anxious, apprehensive, her nerves

most distressingly frayed by the manner of The Three, though she had assured herself at the outset that their mood was a good one. She feared greatly that, feeling nervous she must sound nervous. She felt like any young and newly qualified witch – she, the distinguished Belladonna Agrimony for whom, at the outset of her career, the mighty Merlin had shown himself on more than one occasion. . .

The bright winter sunshine fell upon The Tower and all that fair countryside that spread around it. Even now, at midday, a promise of frost just flushed the sky with green.

"It's dratted cold out here," said Henbane, sharp and sour. "When's she going to let us inside?"

Belladonna bowed and waved The Three towards the door. They crossed the wide terrace and Betony came forward at once to welcome them in.

"See that?" whispered Tarragon to Caraway and Camomile. "Oh look – look!"

The Three were almost to the door – the sun still shone – but their supreme witchhood, their untouchable superiority over all the rest was easily displayed.

For they cast no shadow. Not even Walpurga, Hellebore's cat.

The luncheon table looked magnificent. Old Hemp had surpassed herself. The Singing Blackbird pie was topped with a crust beautifully trimmed with pastry leaves and flowers, and in the middle a nest with eggs in it. In older times, of course, one would have heard the blackbirds jostling and whistling as they waited for the pie to be opened so that they could begin to sing. Today the pie was merely a delicious baked dish. In a tureen alongside, the devilled kidneys swam in hot rich gravy, while the horseradish salad was tastefully served in individual eggshells, crisp and crunchy.

But besides these agreed dishes, Old Hemp had added her own favourites. There was a pheasant cooked in its feathers, a hedgehog baked whole, each spine adorned with a slice of mushroom. While *mouse mousse*, a culinary joke only occasionally met with, brought lip-smacking appreciation from the ancient Henbane. She had not tasted it, she said, since she lodged during her training with the famous Mother Shipton.

"And that time, if you asked me, I'd say the mice were bats!"

The girls all laughed, producing a nice jeering noise that The Three quite obviously approved of — for they looked down the table and nodded their heads and nudged one another. Belladonna relaxed once more. Everything seemed to be going well. She gave Tansy a piercing look and Tansy returned it instantly. That look signalled that the magic should begin.

Tansy turned slightly towards Henbane. The old

witch was stretching out her hand to her glass of Hemlock wine, brim full and darkly bubbling.

Tansy's lips just moved. Her expression was so concentrated that her whole face seemed to grow as small as a pinhead. The others were all watching, waiting. At the head of the table Belladonna loomed larger as Tansy appeared to shrink.

Then out of Henbane's hand, from between her fingers as they closed on the glass, there flew a little bright bird, that circled the table above all their heads, and, twittering, came again to Henbane's hand – to become again a glass of wine.

A barely heard murmur of excitement, a kind of thrumming noise like a string plucked on some ancient instrument, throbbed its way round the table and died. All were otherwise silent, even The Three.

Then Henbane gave an old, thin chuckle.

"Very pretty," she said. "But what sort of a bird was that? Neither wren, robin nor good redwing. Try again, my dear. And this time – let it be a coal-tit."

Tansy trembled. But she felt the others drawing together in support, concentrating so hard that it was a wonder the whole table did not rise in the guise of a flock of pigeons.

Again Henbane stretched out her hand. She gave Tansy a great leering wink and her fingers closed on the glass. It was a moment of truly terrifying suspense. Then – up flew a small pale bird with a neat black head trimmed down the nape with a clear white stripe. This second flight was a double circuit of the table, and then the coal-tit tidily resumed the shape of a wineglass.

It was a little unfortunate that this time the glass was empty, but that did nothing to check the excited applause of the little witches, and the agreeably loud approval of The Three. Betony quickly filled the empty glass, and Belladonna actually heard her own sigh of relief, a sigh that came creaking out of her most painfully. As for Tansy, though pink with pride, she had sat down in a collapsed fashion, and was trembling and shivering with exhaustion. . .

It was at this dramatic moment that Chervil felt a soft movement against her ankle. Musina was trying to attract her attention.

"Well? What is it?" Chervil asked, leaning down as if to pick up her handkerchief.

"She," said Musina. "Trouble. Look out."

She moved away instantly, and Chervil gave a sharp glance around her, *looking out*, as Musina had instructed. But no one was so much as glancing in her direction, they were much too busy babbling about the Flying Wineglass, Hypericum of course recalling an occasion when she had turned a box of a dozen glasses into a crate of hens. . . *Look out*? Of course! Out of the window!

Chervil was facing the window, so that was easy. She looked out – but with a sense of terrible doom that was instantly justified. There, gazing in, was a familiar, totally dejected figure. Oh what could have happened? But in her heart Chervil already knew, for she had foreseen the possibility – the almost certainty – of Miss Agnes Aurelia Pelligrew finishing her book about a young pig in a school blazer and no longer needing her model.

Again, Chervil looked about her. Still everyone was occupied. She must bring Angelica in while The Three were still present – between them they must surely have magic enough to put right the faulty spell.

Chervil rose and without a word to anyone, left the room.

Now everyone relaxed. The green cheese, enormously moonshaped, was placed in the centre of the table and the crackers were handed. There were two kinds of cracker – the ones you eat and the ones you pull. The vintage hemlock having done its work, Hellebore pulled a cracker with Marjoram, and Henbane with Tansy, while Hypericum took one in each hand and offered them to Tarragon and Borage.

Belladonna leant back in her chair. So far, so okay. But the Exhibition of Work had only begun. If only Angelica had been there to take her place with the rest! She had certainly been a very stupid little witch to attempt what was beyond her powers, but she had been the most promising of the lot. It was going to be hard to get over the loss.

Belladonna looked down the table, collecting the glances of Marjoram, Tarragon, Caraway and Spurge. Now for the biggest effort of all – the dreaded tablecloth spell that was called in the Manual *Mensa Clouta*. The young witches gazed back in a fixed and despairing way at the Principal. If they failed, the chaos that was bound to follow was hardly to be thought of. All that food – those dishes – the glasses of wine – the butter. . . No wonder the young witches looked panic stricken. And with horror Belladonna realised that Old Hemp, instead of clearing course by course, had simply added each new dish to what remained of the last. The table was appallingly laden and littered. Gnawed blackbird bones were all over the cloth, the plates were greasy and running with the savoury juices of pheasant and hedgehog. Feathers and quills abounded – the quills having been used by The Three to pick what was left of their teeth, the feathers blowing from side to side almost when any one of them breathed; Tansy's nervous alarm had set up a positive whirlwind.

Belladonna's blood ran colder than it had ever run before. She was appalled to realise how carelessly she had allowed herself to be distracted and lulled by Tansy's success. It was one more proof of her growing tendency to make mistakes. She had actually sat through the meal *enjoying* herself. She groaned inwardly.

But there was nothing to be done. It was too late to make fresh plans. To set about clearing the table at this stage would be to invite suspicion.

Summoning her most powerful and piercing gaze, Belladonna looked towards her pupils. . . And was instantly faced with a further horror. Chervil was missing! She knew she was to be the fifth in the performance of Mensa Clouta, and though that had annoyed her, the fifth member was most necessary to a not very experienced team. Where had the wretched young witch got to?

With a gesture almost of despair, Belladonna gave the prearranged signal and watched her four young pupils move to the four corners of the table. Anyone looking out for it could have seen the magic flashing between them like an electric current arcing over points. . .

The Three were occupied with the final crumbs of the huge cheese, the remaining crackers, the last of the wine. Between munches and gulps they leant near to one another and muttered, as if they were discussing private affairs which none the less would be of enormous interest to all seated at the table.

"Norna coina," murmured Spurge, moving to the north corner of the table.

"Sunta coina," muttered Caraway.

"Yesty coina," breathed Tarragon.

"Wentny coina," sighed Marjoram.

The cloth began to shift. A wine glass tilted – then righted itself. Then silently the cloth slid away, leaving everything else steady, save only for the blackbirds' bones, and the feathers and the quills and the crumbs. But these were quickly pounced on by Walpurga, who had been lying curled up at Hellebore's feet, just waiting for some tiny share of the meal. (Everyone was far too occupied to notice the yowling and spitting that proclaimed the presence under the table of Musina, grabbing her share.)

Belladonna did not speak. Only her eyes flashed her

approval and her appeal to a Lower Power to see the business through successfully to the end.

"Well, well," said Hellebore, without looking up from a spoonful of mouse mousse that she had scraped from the empty bowl. "That was a very nifty performance. Mensa Clouta, if I mistake not. Belladonna, they do you credit."

"So far," remarked Hypericum, somewhat dryly. "What do you think, Henbane?"

"What's that?" Henbane mumbled, nibbling at some of the little bones that had bounced invitingly into her lap. She looked around her, mumbling over the bones, looking quite the oldest witch in the world – and the most mischievous. "Go on – go on!" she cackled. "Proceed, children. What comes next?"

As if she didn't know! The most difficult bit came next. It was now that they needed Chervil – oh where *was* she? – for it was the job of the fifth member of the team to attend to the centre of the cloth and to see that it lay smooth and unrumpled.

But there was no Chervil – no sign of Chervil – no hope that she would return in time. Without her, surely, they were lost.

"Come along, come along," grumbled Hellebore, the one who could not bear to be kept waiting.

There were two ways of replacing the cloth in its original position. It could be drawn in a half-materialised state under the plates and glasses on the table, gradually resuming its right texture and thickness; or it could be sent back in one swift movement. This last was the more impressive way of doing it, earning the spell its familiar nickname of *Now you see it, now you don't.*

It was this form they had decided upon when they practised — but then they had had Chervil's help. Dare they change it, now that her help was removed?

Someone had to take a decision. If Belladonna was signalling instructions they were none of them calm enough to get the message.

"Come, come," said Hypericum testily. "We're all waiting for Phase 2."

"Retorna, rebarba," faltered Spurge, deathly pale as she recalled the fate of a witch who had failed to return the cloth to a king's table. . . "Permisso relanta," she continued, her teeth chattering slightly.

"Cantella cantata," said Caraway.

"Stornta cum stanta," whispered Tarragon.

"Brinto departa!" concluded Marjoram with relief.

Tarragon nudged her violently.

"No, no, Marjoram! *Hinto* — not *brinto*!"

It was too late. The cloth returned, indeed it did, but in what a form! It fell to the table with a clatter like sheets of tin. It crashed on the dishes and the glasses, scattering what food was left — not much — and spinning the whole thing like a cyclone; picking up the four corners, twisting them with a terrible grinding sound, then raising the entire bundle and hurling it against the wall. Spread over the table then was nothing but shattered china, broken glass, bent spoons and forks, knives actually broken off short at the handle.

One by one The Three rose and stood staring across the mess at the four young witches, now huddled very close together, as if each would protect the other from the wrath to come.

In a wild attempt at distraction, Borage, not yet called upon, began disappearing and reappearing with a speed and skill that could hardly have been surpassed by a fully qualified Harridan.

"Now you see *me*!" she cried. "Now you don't!"

And at that Henbane began to cackle. She fell back in her chair, half choked, gasping, so that the other two were bound to attend to her, so that Belladonna had to rush with hemlock in a mug – for all the glasses were broken.

Meanwhile Borage, ready to exhaust herself for the sake of saving the reputation of the Academy, slipped in and out of visibility at increasing and alarming speed, till she became like a spinning top, of which only a blurred image is seen as it goes faster, faster, faster. . .

"Thank you, Borage, that will do," said Belladonna, as Henbane leant her elbows on the shattered table with her hat awry and every elflock on end.

Then, before Borage could wind herself down, the door flew open.

There stood Chervil.

Contrary to every rule in the Manual, she was wearing, without any instruction to do so, her Abracadabra cloak, and she stood holding it out and up like the wings of a bat. Behind it, they all knew instinctively, Something was hidden. Chervil was pale, but her eyes blazed. Surely she was about to produce some magic so sensational that the Academy's name would be inscribed in golden fire for evermore. Breathless, she stood there in the open doorway and seemed unable to speak.

"Presta. . ." she gasped. They almost thought she was going to faint. "Presta – malatesta. . . Lo!"

She dropped her arms and spun to one side. What she had been hiding was revealed for all to see. There stood a small figure, back turned, in a neat blazer and a round school hat. . .

"Angelica!" breathed Tansy. "She's done it! It worked! She's a dear little girl in a blazer!"

"T–t–torno. . ." gasped Chervil.

The figure turned slowly.

There stood a little pig in little girl's clothes, trotters pressed together humbly. The little eyes were lowered, the head bowed, while down those plump pale cheeks two tears ran sad and slow. . .

6. *What Next?*

Long after midnight, Belladonna, Betony, Old Hemp and the pupils, not to mention Musina and Walpurga, were still clearing up the mess caused by the Mensa Clouta disaster. Luncheon had already run on until long after sunset and it had been almost six o'clock by the time Chervil made her dramatic appearance with Angelica.

What happened after that took hours. They had all of them, The Three and Belladonna, set about releasing Angelica. Nothing worked. Books were fetched, covered with dust because the spells they listed had long been replaced by more modern methods. Ingredients were discussed, potions brewed – and so many of them swallowed by poor Angelica that at last she sank down in a stupor and they were obliged to leave her to sleep it off.

At that point The Three, grinding their teeth and shaking their talons, had retired to their rooms. Since then, they had been heard prowling from one room to the other, Henbane alone staying in her own quarters while the other two visited and re-visited, quite clearly hatching between them goodness-knows-what.

"Nice goings on," said Musina to Walpurga, who had stayed downstairs in the hope of snapping up a crumb or two of the debris.

Up went Walpurga's back. She stared wildly, her tail getting bigger all the time.

"Didn't know Belladonna Agrimony had a talking cat?" Musina said with a sneer worthy of Borage.

She was unable to enlarge on this subject. She had stayed silent for a fortnight, hoarding the precious words – then a row yesterday with Old Hemp, something to do with the mouse *mousse*, had used up an alarming number. There had been just enough left to give Chervil Angelica's message – and now she had all but squandered the daily dozen on Walpurga. She had really only been showing off, and was left with only one word in hand. . .

By now everyone was dropping with fatigue. Indeed Tansy had actually gone missing at one point and been discovered curled up and sound asleep in the little cupboard under the sink. One thing kept the young witches going: Belladonna was mysteriously entirely on their side.

"You did well – if that is the word. You did your worst, and that's no contradiction in terms of magic. I was – yes, I must admit it – I was proud of you."

At this even Borage forgot to sneer. As for Camomile and Caraway, they began to cry silently. Even Spurge, though of stronger stuff and older, none the less had tears in her eyes.

"Oh ma'am!" the youngest ones cried. "What will happen to us? What Awful Things are The Three working out for us? Will they turn us into trees? It is winter! How cold we shall be without any leaves!"

They ran to her and stood quite close, huddled together and looking up piteously. It was as if all their training and conditioning had gone into reverse; as if they had returned to their early selves, when they were out in the world and had not even thought of magic. It was almost as if – as if they *loved* Belladonna.

"And then there's poor Angelica!" cried Tansy.

"Oh what did she do that won't come undone?"

"Has she got to stay like that forever?"

"Why can't they un-magic her?"

"Will they ever be able to?"

So cried the young ones. At which Borage, so much more knowing than the rest, asked gloomily, "Do they even want to?"

This brought a terrible outburst of wailing from Tansy and Caraway and Camomile, and Chervil turned, if possible, paler than she was already. It was all so dreadful that Belladonna put out her arms almost as if she would pull them towards her to protect and comfort them.

And, "There, there. . ." she said.

At once, she turned deathly pale, glancing around for Betony. There was Betony, just finishing the washing-up, all suds and steam. . . She smiled at Belladonna.

Then a frightful thing happened, frightful, anyway, in these particular and special circumstances.

Rather shakily, Belladonna smiled back.

At dawn Camomile, the one deputed to look after The Three, took each of them a morning cup of herb tea. It was in fact camomile tea, and she hoped they would like it, as that might very well influence them in her favour. By this it will be seen that Camomile's witchly thoughts were returning to her, and she was making a determined effort to resume evil ways.

The first cup of tea went to Henbane. She was propped up on a lot of pillows and had gone to sleep in her pointed hat, which now rested over one eye. Indeed she was still asleep, her head on her chest, so that her hooked nose and her chin almost met.

"Madam. . ." murmured Camomile.

But Henbane continued a gentle snoring, so Camomile put down the cup on the bedside table and escaped.

Next she went to Hellebore. She tapped rather timidly on this door, and immediately heard Walpurga growl and spit.

"Come in!" called Hellebore, her voice as cold as stone and twice as hard. "About time, too," she snapped, when Camomile entered, brushing nervously past Walpurga's arching back and immense tail. "What's this?"

"It's – it's camomile tea, madam. And I'm Camomile."

Hellebore stared, her eyes much greener today than they had appeared yesterday. Camomile remembered that she should never, never be kept waiting.

"Well?"

"It was – it was a sort of joke, madam."

"If you are able to joke this morning, you have forgotten a great deal more about yesterday than I have."

"Yes, madam," agreed Camomile; and crept away.

She saw how it was to be. Furious at their own inability to un-magic Angelica, The Three were going to bluff their way through by laying all the blame for absolutely everything on Belladonna and her pupils.

Now she had come to Hypericum's door. Very carefully, Camomile tried the handle. It would not budge. She tapped and called out, "Your dawn tea, madam."

Hypericum called back. "Leave it outside."

Camomile bit her lip. She stooped down and put the cup on the floor. It looked dreadful. She ought to have put each cup nicely on a tray, with a bowl of dried elderberries to pretty it up a little. . .

As Camomile straightened up after putting the cup on the floor, she found her left eye on a level with the keyhole. It was left over from the time when The Tower was just an ordinary sort of place – keys and keyholes had little significance nowadays, when doors were shut by other means. The keyhole was blocked, but Camomile blew in a little magic of her own and found she could see beautifully.

Hypericum was sitting on the edge of her bed, busily, even frenziedly tapping at a pocket calculator, then making rapid notes on a large writing pad. Page after page had been used and tossed away. The room was littered with paper torn and paper angrily crumpled into a ball. As Camomile watched, Hypericum threw calculator and all into the middle of the floor, rose and stalked towards the door.

Camomile fled.

"A fine way for guests to behave!" cried Belladonna Agrimony, when she had listened to Camomile's report.

"You didn't invite them," Betony reminded her. "So you can't call them guests. They are VIPs. They can do as they please."

"Oh damn it to Hades," roared Belladonna. "Why has everything gone wrong? They are *plotting*. *What* are they plotting?"

She threw herself back in her chair – she was sitting at her desk – and gnawed so furiously at her goosefeather pen that she was obliged to stop and spit out the fragments.

"Listen!" Betony said.

A crackling sound was coming over the inter-com, though it was not even switched on. Gradually it cleared to a recognisable voice – Henbane, in her most creaking tones.

"We are to consult. Prepare a room for discussion. An announcement will be made. All present. In five minutes." The wicked old voice broke into the faintest of cackles. "Over and out."

Belladonna leapt up.

"Quick, Betony! The dining room! If the table's too knocked about – magic another. A round one would be best – if you can manage that – can you?"

"I think so, mistress."

"Call the pupils! By the Nineteen of the Inner Ring, I find myself quite prepared to stand up to the old hags!"

Within little more than seconds, Belladonna, Betony, the young witches, sad Angelica, were all gathered in the dining room.

It had indeed been necessary to provide a new table – and it was a round one. The little witches ran about twittering and fussing and quite unlike their normal selves – like Camomile they had all tried to get back to their usual ways after their curious behaviour of the night before, but now they had broken down again.

"Oh poor Belladonna Agrimony!" one of them was foolish enough to cry. It must have been Tansy.

"*What*? Miserable child! Pity is not a subject taught in this Academy. Pull yourself together! A little spirited hatred and defiance would best serve this occasion."

"They're coming!" someone cried.

They entered in their usual order – Henbane a little ahead. She was straightening her shabby black skirt – could she have descended by sliding down the handrail? Then came Hypericum, then Hellebore.

"What's this?" demanded Hypericum. "A *round* table? Then who is in charge of the meeting?"

"Why, the most powerful, to be sure," said Belladonna, smooth and guileful. "Pray, Sisters, be seated."

They began jostling a little, their faces black with annoyance. At one point the choice of seats became a kind of musical chairs, with Henbane almost perching on Hypericum's knee. But at last they were settled – Hellebore, Henbane, Hypericum, in that order. Then Belladonna bowing moved smoothly to the seat across the table from Henbane. The bottom, was it? Or the top?

How different a scene from yesterday's in this very room! Then all was celebration, the food and wine so excellent, the company full of nervous anticipation and excitement. Today these sensations were mixed together like any old potion, and the result was sheer stark panic. What had The Three in store for Belladonna Agrimony's Academy for Young Witches? Would they be closed down? Disbanded? Deported? Turned out into the snow? (This last seemed not impossible, for beyond the windows they could see a December sky that showed as black as the looks of The Three.)

Henbane spoke:

"First I have to inform you that we shall be gone from here before the sun peers at the meridian." She looked round the table, grinning nastily. "No tears for that, I see. Let me say, Sister Belladonna, that in spite of certain – occurrences – we have decided to find no fault with the Academy's level of achievement. The disaster of Mensa Clouta was easily understandable and in different circumstances might have been averted. We are therefore agreed in drawing an invisible veil over yesterday's memory. We shall proceed to the original purpose of our visit."

Her creaking old voice died and she began to cough. The pupils looked from one to the other. What about Angelica? Why had Henbane not spoken of her? Were they washing their wicked hands of her, abandoning her to her piggish fate?

Henbane was still choking a bit, so Hypericum took over.

"Today," she announced, "there are many changes in our world as we have known it. We must move with the times or face a threat of disaster. It is up to us to fall in with the many new customs we observe about us. It has been decided, therefore, that from the first term of the Sorcerer's Year – that is, of course, the term of the Summer Solstice – this Academy, with its sister establishment over the Border, will be required to open its doors to mixed education."

A ripple of dismay – was it? – ran round the round table.

"That will mean a fifty-fifty ratio of boys to girls," Hellebore put in, leaning back in her chair with Walpurga on her lap, and observing with obvious satisfaction the varying expressions on the faces before her.

Belladonna spoke.

"Never!"

Borage was working it out. What was a fifty-fifty ratio? Did it mean that fifty girls would have fifty boy friends? Or perhaps that each girl would have fifty boy friends? Quite an idea, really. But it might mean that every boy would have fifty girl friends – which was a very different kettle of fish.

"Never!" Belladonna announced for the second time. Then for force added a third, "Never!"

"We leave the idea with you," Hypericum said, easily enough.

"But it is bound to seem to you a choice of evils," said Hellebore.

"Either open your doors to young wizards," screeched Henbane, "or close them altogether!"

"But why? Why?"

"It is called progress, Sister."

"It can't be progress to close the place down."

"We shall open another, of course."

"You mean – the same?"

"The same only different," said Hellebore in a thoroughly satisfied tone.

"We shall now be on our way," said Hypericum.

"Leaving you to consider your future arrangements," concluded Henbane.

They rose. They seemed suddenly to have grown immensely tall. They lifted their arms in gestures of farewell, and their huge embroidered cloaks fell back to reveal the many signs and symbols woven into the linings.

"Ah!" said Hellebore, pausing as she turned to the door, "I almost forgot. We need another broomstick. You will, of course, supply it."

Belladonna frowned.

"But you have your broomsticks, ladies," Betony said.

"Yes, yes, of course. But we need one for Angelica."

"Angelica?"

"The little pig-girl. Isn't that her name?"

A terrible buzz ran round and over the table, then died into a silence even more awful.

"We are bound for Scotland," Hypericum said briskly.

"We are to give a Course on Transformations to the students there," explained Hypericum.

"Followed by a World Tour," added Henbane.

Belladonna could hardly find words. She stuttered something about not knowing what they were talking about. . . Angelica, meanwhile, seemed in a kind of trance, waving her trotters feebly, turning first to one then to another of the young witches, as if for help.

"We intend," said Hypericum, "having tested all permutations and combinations available to the best computers and learning that for this particular transformation there can be no reversal, we intend to take Angelica with us as a demonstration model."

Horror struck them all. They cried out wildly, rushing to Angelica and surrounding her defiantly as she collapsed utterly.

Belladonna sprang furiously to her feet. She went close to Henbane and they stood with their heads lowered, shaking their elf-locks and flashing their eyes at one another, clenching and unclenching their talons.

"A broomstick for Angelica, if you please," snarled Henbane.

"Magic your own!"

The Three cackled as one. "You know that is impossible. A magicked broomstick will always suffer from birch-fatigue. We have to fly the length of England. We would not fancy touching down on the motorway!"

"I have no broomstick to spare," Belladonna said, stepping back slightly and resuming her dignity. "You can hardly expect me to hand over my own trusty vehicle, or Betony hers. My pupils have not yet aspired to flying-brooms. They work only with the simplest form."

She paused a second, as The Three turned to one another and spat out a few words. Then she said,

"There is, however, a moderately skilled broommaker on the far side of the forest. I suggest you seek what you need in his workshop."

The Three looked from one to the other. They moved together, leaning into a whispering triangle of pointed hats. At last they separated; they had made a decision.

"Very well," said Hellebore. "We are agreed. This man shall supply what is needed."

"Let Betony go to him at once and purchase the best he has," ordered Hypericum.

"Until then," said Henbane, "We shall wait in our rooms."

7. *'Sliver'd in the moon's eclipse. . .'*

Betony returned from the broom-maker.

"He has no finished broom for sale."

"What? What's that mean?"

"He must cut fresh birch. He'll do it by tomorrow."

She was speaking to Hellebore, who could not endure to be kept waiting. Hellebore snarled and all but spat, but there was nothing she could do to hurry on the broom. She swished about her room, showing her teeth. At one moment Betony stepped back hastily, for it seemed that Hellebore was just beginning to breathe fire.

Betony left the furious witch. She dropped down swiftly and quietly through the core of The Tower and found the others huddling miserably in the basement.

They had gone there to get as far as possible from the Baleful Influences wafting out from the rooms of The Three on the top floor.

The little witches were listening for the twentieth time at least to the story Angelica had to tell. It came out in grunts and snorts but was none the less enthralling for that. How she had been dared by Borage — how she had pondered — how the fatal word 'pigtail' had seemed to give her just what she needed. How she had gone to the kitchen, seized the pig's entrails and tail and fled with them into the deep forest.

"I did think the spell had worked," Angelica told them between most melancholy snuffles. "Then I saw my — my trotters. I ran fast to that pond in Plashy Wood and looked in — and there was my face, and it was a little pig's face!"

Then she told of Miss Pelligrew and everything being so splendid.

"Only not even Agnes Aurelia Pelligrew could go on and on writing about a pig in a blazer. One day she said I could surely turn myself into a baby elephant in a ballet skirt. I couldn't — I couldn't!"

While they all listened and made wild and wilder suggestions about what must be done, Belladonna sat slumped in a chair by the stove — whether upstairs or downstairs, in bed or living rooms, witches never, never have open fires.

"Well?" she asked, as Betony came in.

"He has to make a broom."

At that Belladonna looked up sharply.

"None in stock?"

"None. He must cut boughs. The broom must be specially made."

Betony looked hard at Belladonna, as if waiting for a reply. But Belladonna stayed silent. She seemed to be thinking with great difficulty. Then she suddenly sat up, crying –

"How long?"

"This time tomorrow, mistress."

"Then – there could still be time – if only we could discover what to do. And since They were not able to..."

She rose and began to pace the room as Hellebore had paced, but without any signs of breathing fire – though she could, of course, have done so had she chosen. As it was, the little witches could all but hear the re-fuelled thoughts of their Principal whirring and thumping, thudding and clattering as she got them into motion once more.

"Think! Think!" she cried to Angelica. "Try to recall the Order of Spelling!"

"I've tried! I've tried! I can't!"

"Did the change come before the final word – or after?"

"I can't remember!" wailed Angelica.

"How did you employ the Vital Ingredient? The pig's tail, girl! Did you cook it and eat it? Was the fire of alder or willow? Or did you bury it with a sprig of rue and a root of hyssop? Or did you wave it in circles? In circles round your head? If so – was it in your left hand or your right? How were your thumbs placed – over or under? *You must remember, Angelica*!"

Angelica could only whine, "I've forgotten. I was very upset. . ."

"They have scrambled her lines," Betony murmured to Belladonna. "They have thought of everything. They have called up the Guardians and the Messengers. There are Sorcerers' Circles laid, one after the other after the other, from the steps outside the front door to the hollies and even beyond."

"You mean we are prisoners?"

"We are prisoners. In the last Circle they have set a Gate with Guardians. They let me through because I was on an errand for The Three. None other would get by."

"There must be a way," growled Belladonna. "*There must be a way*! Think again – all of you! Concentrate! Concentrate!"

But the more they tried the more confused they all became. The Three had stuffed The Tower with magic, for their whole purpose was to keep Angelica as she was. The young witches were hopelessly confused by the power released into every corner. They could not hope to stand against it.

But what of Belladonna?

What indeed? Could she, descendant of a long and distinguished line, acknowledged a great teacher, immensely skilled in the most subtle enchantments – could even she hope to defeat The Three. Once, perhaps. But now? That uncomfortable kindness she experienced at times, a positive pain round the heart, as if it had begun to lose its hardness, told its own tale. If she went on at this rate she could not hope to last much longer.

The pain was there now as she considered Angelica's fate if they could not get her unmagicked. She would be the wretched slave of The Three. Their lecture tours were famous, for they covered the world. They were constantly invited to speak at distant colleges, academies of one sorcery or another, secret Orders of Enchantment beyond the seas, beyond the mountains, even deep in that strange territory under the earth, where an audience would gather in some great cavern, while The Three lectured by torchlight to the sound of mysterious underground torrents falling into vast underground lakes. Poor Angelica would be dragged around, set up to be stared at and discussed – and not as an object lesson in how the thing should be done, but how it should *not* be done. . .

This was indeed a solemn moment in the long career

of Belladonna Agrimony. She had to succeed now if never again.

Then it was tomorrow. The situation remained unchanged. Betony went again to the broom maker. Peering from their basement window, only half of it above ground, the rest of them watched as she paused at invisible barriers and then crossed them by unspoken permission. They waited and waited for her return, Borage forgetting to sneer, Chervil setting aside her ambitions, each and every one of them somehow strangely different from her usual witchly self.

Once again, Betony returned empty-handed.

This time she spoke to Hypericum.

"He regrets the delay. He has no withy for the clish."

Hypericum glared. "No *what*? For the *which*?"

"No stripped willow, madam. For the binding of the boughs."

"What then?" snarled Hypericum.

"This time tomorrow. He swears it. The withy must lie overnight in running water. . ."

She watched Hypericum shudder at the words 'running water'. A very small smile just touched the left corner of Betony's mouth.

"Tomorrow, then. And let there be no more blunders," Hypericum snapped.

As before, Betony descended to find the rest.

"Well?"

"Mistress, we have one more day and one more night."

"Betony, Betony, I have been through all my great store and savings of enchantment – and still I can see no way to unmagick Angelica. And if she cannot be unmagicked – then for sure they will take her. For they are the Most Powerful of Witches."

"They think they are," said Betony, "and tell us so. Perhaps we are magicked into believing it?"

"Ah – that's easy talk. . ."

"Mistress," said Betony, standing close and almost whispering, "there are older powers than ours or theirs within this very grove."

"The yew trees! The great gnarled wisdom they hold in trunk and branch and twig. . . Do you speak of the yew trees, Betony?"

"I do speak of them, mistress."

"But the Gates – and the Guardians – and the Sorcerers' Circles – ? How should we even reach the yew trees when The Three have hemmed us in?"

"Oh mistress, dear Belladonna Agrimony," said Betony, soft and softer, "there is something you have overlooked."

"I never overlook –" began Belladonna sharply. Then she hesitated and said quietly, "*What* have I overlooked?"

"Between today and tomorrow," said Betony, "between night and morning, light and dark, then and now – the moon is to go into total eclipse."

Belladonna was silent, looking at Betony in a puzzled way.

"Eclipse. . .? But the calendar. . . How could I have overlooked such a thing? And surely – the phase is wrong?"

"Right or wrong," answered Betony, steady and unruffled, calm and positive, "at midnight precisely, the moon will be entirely hidden."

"Is it possible?"

"All things are possible to a firm purpose, mistress."

"Then," said Belladonna, recognising at last that here was a thing that should not be questioned, "tell me your thoughts, my good Betony."

"We need each to pluck a slip of yew in those instants when the dark is down. If there should be both berry and flower, then we are in a fair way to succeed. But you know how little time will be ours."

Belladonna gripped Betony's arm tightly.

"You have thought deeply – deeply and well."

"I think as you think, mistress," Betony replied.

Then she stepped back and bowed slightly, leaving Belladonna to make what she might of the words.

In those few moments of time when light is altogether absent, moments of total eclipse known as Utter Dark, all power is withdrawn. Warm-blooded creatures scarcely find breath for living through such a time. Plant life is arrested. The world is suspended in a state of terrible apprehension. . . . So far, light has always returned, slowly, painfully but with great beauty, restoring life to all that has feared to lose it forever.

It is known to a few only, such as Belladonna and her Sisters, and a poet or two through the ages, that when the power is withdrawn by the ending of light, it passes into those ancient sentinels, the yews. Therefore of all things magic, most magical is the green slip of yew, or the sliver peeled from the bark with a silver knife, taken at the moment of eclipse. This was Belladonna's utmost need, that could succeed where all else had failed. As she issued her instructions to the young witches, they grew pale.

"There will be little more than seconds for our purpose. Each one of us must take one slip or sliver and no more. Though the Circles will slacken and the Guards fall into trance, they will recover themselves on the instant that the moon reappears. Also, we shall ourselves be influenced by the withdrawal of light and power. We shall be like walkers through water, stepping with difficulty."

The day passed slowly, very slowly indeed. They barely knew how to occupy themselves. At intervals there came down orders for food and drink from The

Three closeted above.

"Wine for our sister Henbane – a bottle of that hemlock will suit her."

"Three bowls of poad-milk and a herb loaf."

Or, less politely still, "Send the dinner! Are we to be kept waiting for ever? Where's Camomile? Send her about her duties. We are your guests and must be attended. *All this bodes ill for the future of the Academy*."

Once Walpurga slipped padding down the spiral stair and stood at the door, as impatient as Hellebore herself at being kept waiting.

"Let her out," said Musina, smirking. "Even a witch's cat cannot stay indoors for ever."

Then she, too, lashed her tail – once again she had stupidly spent her day's supply of words in one rush...

Now it was dusk... Now it was dark. They crowded at the meagre window, saw the moon rise, watched its light increase. The shadows of the immense yews were cast forward, long and black, then as the moon rose higher the shadows began to shorten. It was a most perfect night, chill but not bitter, no breath of wind, a hint of frost. A magical night, most truly – but strangely so, as any one of them was bound to see. Was not one most important subject of their studies the Calendar? Why – it was almost the first thing they learnt about, so vital were stars and planets and comets and eclipses to the proper practice of the witch's art.

So Chervil said to Borage under her breath, "The phase is wrong."

"I have seen and forgotten," answered Borage, turning away.

Then Chervil muttered to Spurge and Tansy, "This is madness. The phase is wrong. I don't understand."

"Hush!" whispered clever Tansy.

"Be silent!" hissed Spurge.

Chervil frowned and looked flustered. It took a full moon to eclipse totally, and this moon would not be full for two nights to come; and even then there was no prediction of eclipse.

But as they waited, uncertain, full of doubts that shamed them into silence, gradually they took heart from the firmness of Belladonna and Betony. The crowded basement room became crowded, then, with growing courage, with a sense of strong purpose. At last even Chervil was won over and it was she who said to Angelica that soon she would be herself again.

"Of course. I know that," said Angelica, with a confident grunt.

Then as they waited they saw the first faint nibble of shadow along the moon's smooth rim.

"Take The Three their bedtime possets, Camomile," said Belladonna.

She had set three goblets on a tray and filled them from the pitcher in which such drinks were always brewed. Now she bent over the tray, and with a spiralling movement of both hands she caused the drink at once to bubble hotly; steam and froth heaved at the rims. Then into each goblet was set one leaf of bay, one blade of rosemary, with a third ingredient which is secret. She murmured under her breath as she did so,

"Lullorum, lulloram; totantum cum snorum. . ."

"Camomile!" came Hellebore's impatient voice. "It is bedtime! Bring us our drinks!"

"Go quickly," Belladonna said to the trembling Camomile. "If possible, wait while they drink. It will help us if we are sure. . ."

The Three were together in Henbane's room. With alarm Camomile saw that the curtains were undrawn, the moon clearly seen.

"About time," snarled Hellebore.

"Get a move on or the drink will lose its head," snapped Hypericum.

"I can't abide a flat posset and I can do with a drink," cackled Henbane.

Quickly Camomile handed the goblets, bowing to each lady most politely as she did so. She watched them sniff at the goblets and felt her knees knocking. But they all smacked their lips appreciatively.

"A toast!" cried Henbane. "Bad befall, within and without!"

"Bad befall!" echoed Hellebore.

"Within and without!" concluded Hypericum.

They drank.

Camomile fled. As she closed the door behind her swift as light, she heard Hypericum cry out –

"The moon! Lucifer save us! The moon!"

For an instant Camomile stood rigid. Then she heard a thud, and another, and another, as the goblets fell to the ground. Then she heard a rustling and a struggling as The Three subsided among them. She crouched to peer through the keyhole, but it was blocked. She blew in a little magic and saw clearly The Three stretched on the ground in a series of ungainly heaps.

She stayed a second longer, waiting for some move or sound. Nothing stirred.

"Snorum totorum," she murmured contentedly; and flew down the stairs without thinking. She had never actually flown before.

Utter Dark lay over the grove. The yews, so black by day, seemed now to loom out of the shadows. They drew the power to themselves, remembering the last time, anticipating the next, confident they would survive for ever. . .

Belladonna, Betony, all the young witches save Angelica, left behind to wring her trotters till they returned, struggled with the dark that seemed to pluck the breath from their bodies, the strength from their limbs. No one spoke. They moved as best they could, striving to keep their feet off the ground, their hands stretched out, their fingers groping. Slowly they got the measure of their difficulties and, as their purpose strengthened, so also they began to conquer those difficulties. None hindered them. They passed through the Circles. The Guardians were nowhere. The Gate was down. . .

They had reached the yews. There was no time for a choice of easy picking, and the yew resisted hard. It pulled back from their groping, grabbing fingers, snapped back into their faces, dragging away from their hands so hard that they were burnt and blistered by the contact.

The young witches began to gasp and flutter, for the time was going over so fast they feared they might never get back to The Tower before the light returned and with it the strength of all those many spells that had been laid wickedly entangled about the grove and The Tower.

"Hurry!" cried Belladonna, sheathing her silver knife and slipping a long splinter into her pocket. She moved from one to the other. "Remember – each of us must pluck. Is that you, Caraway? Hurry, child."

"Got it!" gasped Caraway, and tumbled backwards clutching a berried twig.

"Return!" Belladonna ordered. "Return now – all

return! It is almost too late!"

A shaving of moon was reappearing from the shadow, so bright in contrast that it was almost blinding.

"Whhoooooosshhhh!" cried Belladonna – and seemed to scoop them all up and drive them forward. On and on they skimmed ahead of her, persistently tripping as the strength of the Circles began to revive, gasping with fright for The Tower seemed far ahead – too far for them ever to regain its shelter.

Then they were at the door and it opened to let them through, Belladonna standing sentinel, her great cloak outstretched until the last was safe over the threshhold. Then she fled inside herself, slamming the door and bolting it with a curse too terrible to be set down here.

Above The Tower the crooked moon slid with almost a smile from its strange eclipse. Betony looked up through the window and maybe she smiled back. . .

For the first time in her long, long witch-hood, Belladonna Agrimony fainted clean away.

There was little time, however, to waste on the vapours. The yew must be counted over, arranged in its perfect circle with each pupil guarding her own plucking, Angelica set at the exact centre. A draught of feverfew and agrimony, her personal herb, quickly revived Belladonna and she began snapping out orders.

"My wand, Betony. My pentacle. My amulet. My cup.

My sword. My knife."

When these things had been brought and the circle perfected, Belladonna wrapped her great cloak about her – her Abracadabra cloak, that is – and began carefully and quietly the intense and powerful spell that was to return Angelica to her natural form.

8. *Merrily, Merrily...*

High in their rooms at the top of The Tower, The Three were waking. It was the beginning of the winter dawn, the moon brilliant in the west, the eastern horizon just glimmering, the forest rising out of shadow, its creatures shaking off the night's chill that had frosted not only grass and bush and tree, but even the backs of the crouching deer. To the north, as yet unseen, great rolls and curls of snow cloud were gathering.

First Hypericum woke, then Hellebore, seconds later. Last of all Henbane, rising with difficulty from the hard floor on which they had all drunkenly slumbered.

They looked at one another, for once bewildered. Then the last fumes of their bedtime drink blew away and the truth flashed upon them.

"Magicked!" they cried in fury, speaking for once in perfect unison.

They rose. They stamped and prowled. They planned and they plotted.

"Revenge!" cried Hellebore.

"Revenge!" cried Hypericum.

"Just so," said Henbane in a voice faint and hoarse with hatred.

Then Hypericum spoke, sending her voice ringing down through The Tower, with that skill in communication which Belladonna had never accomplished.

"We are leaving."

"Bring Angelica."

"And bring Angelica's broom!" screeched Henbane. "We're off!"

The voices sounded out in the basement.

What a scene of despair they fell upon!

The spell had worked only in part. The pig's trotters had been replaced by hands and feet – but Angelica was still far more a little pig than a little girl and it seemed as if Belladonna had exhausted all her powers.

In the intensity of her concentration, in the hugeness of the magic she had summoned, the yew had withered, its dark spears shrivelling and falling, so that the floor was littered. Still at the centre of the now ruined circle, Angelica crouched exhausted and in despair, her pig's face hidden in her hands and even the neat bow tying her pigtail half undone and crumpled. The young witches, pale and feverish, huddled in miserable groups. Belladonna herself had fallen back in her chair, her cloak tossed away, her hands trailing, her eyes shut and her feet sprawling in weariness.

No one spoke.

Then came the voices of The Three. . .

"No! No!" wailed Angelica.

The pupils groaned and sighed, too worn out to make any stronger protest.

"Mistress. . ." murmured Betony, standing over Belladonna.

Belladonna opened her eyes. As she did so a strange, an almost terrible thing occurred. Two tears ran from the right eye, then one from the left.

"Oh mistress," said Betony again. "Have you remembered?"

The word brought a faint stirring among the rest. Angelica looked up — as if to remember was to succeed though there might have been first a hundred failures.

"We are waiting!" came Hellebore's furious voice.

Belladonna rose. She caught her tears on the ends of her fingers and pressed the fingers against Angelica's little pig cheeks.

"The crystal flask!" she cried. "Bring me the crystal flask, Betony! Waste no time!"

It seemed as if Betony did not even leave the room

before she was handing to Belladonna that crystal flask in which, so long a time ago, her own infant tears had been collected, and stored until they rattled like tiny pearls.

"I said they'd come in handy!" Belladonna cried.

She pulled out the sapphire stopper and held up the flask.

A faint seething came from within the flask. The pearls began to melt and mould together and then there rose a mist, fine and graceful, that spiralled and wreathed about them, seeping into their eyes and noses, a powerful fume, heady and thrilling and full of inexpressibly brilliant magic.

"Crystala potenta," murmured Belladonna. "O fumor anticipatator! Labor! Labor! Salvinta! Puella ni porcinnabar!"

As the words of the spell, humble and faltering as they were, fell on the despair and silence that had preceded them, the little witches began to revive. They stirred and jumped up, and then as the wonderful magic of those melting pearls fell upon them all, they began to leap and to dance, laughing and calling out in delight.

"Oh why couldn't we see!" cried Tansy, actually throwing herself on Belladonna, clasping her round the waist and hugging her. "It's her pigtail! Oh look – look! It's the real pig's tail and we never noticed! Cut it off! Oh quickly, quickly! Take your magic knife and cut it off!"

But as the last wisp of magic rose from the flask, leaving it empty of all that it had contained, the pigtail fell off of its own accord, ribbon and all, and instantly Angelica began to change.

Everyone was jumping about wildly, forgetting all about The Three and their awful commands that had rung out so harsh and imperious. There was clapping and cheering as the pigginess faded and faded and finally vanished. There at last stood Angelica herself, the wickedest one, beginning to smile, to run about and kick her legs in the air, to spin and to swing around, seizing first one and then another of her fellow pupils, whirling them about; and laughing so joyously that soon every one of them had joined in — Borage and Spurge, Caraway and Camomile, Tarragon and Tansy and Marjoram. Even Chervil. And Betony. Even — even Belladonna. . .

"Bring us Angelica!" came Henbane's screaming and furious voice.

"Come and get me!" Angelica shouted back, in her own, little-girl-witch's most defiant tones. "Come and get me! *You Old Hags*!"

Then all over The Tower a terrible silence fell.

Down in the basement they waited for something to happen. What? No one could have said. The silence held. There was no movement above. No voice. No opening door. Nothing. Nothing of such intensity that it almost made a sound of its own.

Then Betony said, "Listen!"

There came a great swishing and a fluttering and a huge thud as the main door of The Tower was flung back and The Three came forth. Barely pausing on the terrace, they mounted their broomsticks and took flight.

Below, clustered round that small window, Belladonna and the rest gazed upward. They saw The Three very distinctly, for the morning by now filled the sky, though the curling snow clouds had quite obscured the sun. The sound of The Three in flight continued, a rushing, rather terrible sound, as of wings – not the huge wings of swans or eagles, but rather the thousand thousand wings of small birds driven out and twittering in fear as they flew.

The Three did not immediately sweep away northward, as might have been expected. They began swooping and hovering round and about The Tower, coming so dangerously near that it was easy to see Hellebore's disagreeable features, Hypericum's piercing eyes, Henbane's nutcracker nose and chin – even Walpurga's expression of contemptuous superiority.

Suddenly they soared high, high, and everyone in the basement moved, running to the door and up the stairs and out on to the terrace, as if to speed them on their way with shaking fists.

Yet again The Three returned, and in a heady corkscrew, in close formation, they dropped almost to the ground, then swept again upward, round and round The Tower three times to widdershins and no more. As they went they laughed, huge witches' laughs, full of evil intention and bitter malice.

At last they rose high above The Tower, higher, higher, till their flowing cloaks looked no bigger than the wings of bats. Gradually the distance received them. The clouds closed over them like water closing on a stone. . .

"Mistress," shrieked Betony. "Quick! Quick!"

She had turned back as if to re-enter The Tower. At her cry the rest turned, too. As they did so the big door of The Tower closed with a mighty thud, while up and down the building shutters slammed and clattered on every window, leaving blankness to face out across the forest. First the basement window was shuttered, then the ground floor, and so on in tidy rotation up to the very pinnacle, where Belladonna Agrimony's study, Tower Top, looked with eight separate eyes upon the surrounding countryside. At last those eyes, too, had closed. . .

Belladonna rushed forward, and all the rest surged after her — to rattle the door handle and bang and shove, then to rush round to the door at the far side, and there also to rattle and bang and shove. But all was tight shut. There was no way of entering. All cries of "Portnabulum oventibus" fell like tossed gravel to the ground. There was, quite simply, no way in.

Trying hard not to shake with fury and distress, Belladonna went once more to the main door, unable to believe what she knew too well must be true.

A notice had appeared on the door. There was just one word:

DEPART!

They stood together, reading the word over and over, as if they might find in its repetition a different, more hopeful meaning.

But there is just one meaning to the word *Depart* – it is merely a grander way of saying GO!

Belladonna gathered her great cloak about her and turned from the door of The Tower. She strode down the few steps from the terrace and the rest followed. Nothing hindered them. The Sorcerers' Circles had been withdrawn; the Guardians were gone; no Gate remained. . .

It began to snow.

This is quite a large forest, though not as large as some, and there are many places in it where such as Belladonna might expect to find a lodging. There are groves of holly as well as yew, and beech woods whose oldest trees offer in themselves an enchanted habitation.

The animals are friendly for they recognise magic when they smell it.

That morning the snow fell gently and steadily, dry and capricious, whirling and drifting. It settled first on the copper and bronze of fallen beech leaves, but very soon it had outlined a million fronds of dead red bracken and impaled itself on every gorsey thorn. The increasing whiteness and purity might, perhaps, have been expected to irritate any decently trained witch. But since the unstoppering of the crystal flask such changes had taken place that the scene greatly pleased the eyes of Belladonna and the young witches of her Academy. The mood as a whole was extraordinary.

Belladonna was still striding ahead of the rest, confident of where she was going without precisely knowing what her destination would be. Layers of old blackness continued to peel from her heart, her spirit increasingly lightened. Sometimes at her heels, sometimes at her side, sometimes darting into the lead, Musina, restored to almost kittenish ways, ran and leapt and pranced.

But of all those following after Belladonna, none was so wild and noisy as Angelica. Perhaps it was watching her, saved from a dreary fate, so beautifully restored to her own self, that caused Belladonna to hum under her breath as she strode along like a general leading his army, her cloak blowing wide and speckled with snow flakes, her hat on the back of her head. Then between

the hums she sang a few notes, then a whole snatch of tune burst from her. One of the others – Camomile had a pleasant voice – picked up the tune, discovered its words and began to sing out bold and clear.

One by one they joined in the song, not so loudly at first, it being some long time since they had indulged in such pleasantry, but then louder, bolder, merrily, stepping out to the rhythm, sweeping their way through the snowy forest to some place they knew they must find – the pupils following Betony, Betony following Belladonna, Belladonna after Musina – and Musina, quite suddenly, led by a light-stepping young roe buck. What the deer followed none might see – maybe some ghost whose usual way was along this path and through this wood, who recognised their song and soundlessly joined in. . .

"Through the Forest, which our place is,
Moth-wing snow blown in our faces;
Dark must come while still we travel –
Seeing how our fortunes ravel,
Knowing how our spellings tangle,
How some dwelling we must fangle. . .
  Hie us fast, then, to some shelter,
  Helter skelter, helter skelter. . .

"Through the Forest we must hurry
Without sign of nervous scurry,
Without fear of coming night-time,
Without doubt about the right time
When with gentlest magic power
We'll enchant the waiting hour,
  Tame it, chain it, stake our pleasure
  To this single, singing measure. . .

"Through the Forest bravely scramble,
Under birch and over bramble,
Keenly cheerful, singing, tripping,
In and out of shadow slipping –
When the time comes we shall know it,

Trees and creatures all shall show it. . .
Follow after Belladonna,
Heaping every hope upon her. . .
Belladonna! Belladonna!
We, your pupils, do you honour!
Belladonna. . . . Belladonna. . ."

As the last notes of the last verse died away and they were all wondering whether it would be a good idea to start again, they came to an opening in the trees. There the deer paused, framed in that entry, as clever as any living deer at looking like one painted and framed and hung on a wall. The creature tossed its head, then stepped aside, and with barely a movement of the seedling birch growing here in great tangles and plaitings of useful cover, it vanished.

The rest ran forward. For a second they wondered if they had travelled in a circle and arrived back at The Tower. But what they saw was an ancient windmill, that maybe only the deer could have led them to, it was so secret. Of its several hundred years of existence it must surely have spent a hundred entirely hidden from view, as the forest changed its shape, as time took forest people to other places, making other paths, leaving what had once been a place of bustle and trade, so that at last it was forgotten. The mill's sails were mere skeletons. Its sides in many places gaped and bulged. Its door hung creaking on one hinge. . .

"This is the place," said Belladonna.

"Here?" they all cried, the least dismayed.

"It only needs a little magicking," Belladonna assured them. "A few hours and a few spells from now – you'll hardly know the place."

"Will there really be room for us all?"

"We can build on, Marjoram."

"What shall we do for water?"

"Use your eyes, Borage – there's a good spring bubbling not five yards from your right toe."

"What shall we do for furniture?"

"Caraway – have you forgotten everything you've been taught?"

"Furniture spells are easy, aren't they, ma'am?" cried Angelica. "I can do lots!"

"I think, Angelica," said Belladonna firmly, "That we had better do without your particular skills, at any rate for a time."

"Let's go in," said Betony.

Musina had already entered the mill and now emerged with a mouse in her mouth. But she seemed disinclined to eat it, and after putting it down and patting it a couple of times, she watched tolerantly as it ran off into the snow-covered grass. . .

Furnishing by magic is much the same as furnishing by money, except that it is easier. By nightfall they had sealed all the holes in the walls, wished a new roof over the old one, stopped the sails creaking, and made the place quite comfortable. Stoves glowed warm on each of the three floors and hammocks had been slung for bedtime. Tansy had magicked some very pretty curtains, and Chervil some chairs – rather rickety, it is true, but the best she could manage with her limited talents. There was a very nice table with room for all of them, and some lovely china and glass. They had not done so well with knives and forks, since these need strong and malicious magic. The whole crowd of them were feeling so mild and considerate and easy-going that they were obliged to be content with the sort of plastic cutlery used on picnics. It was a small disadvantage, however, amid all the rest.

Musina had joined in, performing a little spell of her own, and obtaining some delicious fresh milk to drink. As Betony said, it was sheer saucery.

Suddenly a voice sounded up the stairway.

"I see you go and you never give me a thought," grumbled Old Hemp.

She climbed up to be greeted. They had indeed forgotten all about her in the flurry. Musina rubbed against her ankles and borrowed a few of tomorrow's word allowance in order to greet her. The rest helped her to unload the huge great bundle she had carried on her back, as she followed their fading footsteps in the snow, all the way through the deep forest from The Tower to The Mill. The bundle was full of useful things like jelly moulds and screwdrivers, and even a jar of tomagic chutney.

"Now let me be," said Old Hemp, shoving off the lot of them. "I'll get to me kitchen and see what'll summon itself up for supper." She paused a second to give Angelica a playful shove. "And tomorrer, if I'm not mistook, there'll be a sweet tasty piece o' pork for dinner!"

Perhaps it was the best meal they had ever tasted. All the misery over Angelica, the horrible experience with The Three, the terror of the moment when they had sped through the Utter Dark, the despair when they failed in their purpose – all this just melted from their minds. And with it melted much that they had been so studiously and so skilfully taught. Like Malevolence, and Evil Intent; like Hard Thoughts and Sneers and every sort of Nasty Behaviour. Sneers were now smiles, and as they grew gradually sleepy after the wonderful supper supplied by Old Hemp, the good old Wizard of Nosh, they felt just like a lot of dear little girls in clean nighties, with hair smooth-brushed and shining, all ready and waiting for some delightful bedtime story to be read to them by dear Betony or darling Belladonna. . .

And now it was night. The pupils swung sleepily in their hammocks, Musina sat curled and purring by the stove, Betony had taken out her knitting.

"Well," said Belladonna, "just one little job more, then I'm for dreamland."

She looked quickly at Betony, fearing she had heard a small snort of laughter; but Betony just sat there knitting away.

Belladonna went down the steps and out into the bitter night. The snow had stopped falling. It was freezing. There hung the moon, putting out the stars with its brilliance. Belladonna glanced at the moon and then looked quickly away. She shook her head in a puzzled manner. The less said about that eclipse the better. Some very unusual magic had been summoned up. It had little to do, Belladonna suspected, with the heaped-up wisdom of the ancient yew trees. It was Betony who held the key to this secret, a secret that might never be told.

For in Betony there rested a magic as powerful in its own way as Merlin's. It had no name that Belladonna cared to give it. It was a magic born in many and too often carelessly thrown away. Belladonna herself had possessed it once, exchanged it boldly for her witchhood – and thought no more of it till Betony came mysteriously to change her life.

She stood a second or two, trying to think but not

succeeding very well. Far away, then suddenly much nearer, she heard a vixen crying after a mate, and then a pair of owls swished out of the crowding trees, swished past her and swished out of sight. She heard them calling in a gossipy way as they went.

She had already arranged for a board to hang on the door of the mill, and now she took it and hammered it soundlessly into place. Then she stood back and looked at it in the moonlight.

The Academy for Young Witches. Principal: Belladonna Agrimony.

Having regard to what had been going on since they reached this new home, the wording on the board seemed vaguely unsuitable. She wondered how she might rearrange it, for there was a hint of falsity in the words now. Should she change *Young Witches* to *Young Ladies*? No — that really did seem to be going it a bit, as Old Hemp might say. . . But what else? Perhaps it should read differently altogether? Say *Home for Retired Witches.*

Belladonna chuckled very quietly. The words, she decided, had better stay as they were. No spell lasts for ever, and who could tell how long it might be before, just as Angelica had regained her own shape, they might all recover their essential witchiness?

Belladonna yawned a bit. She went inside, closing the door carefully and quietly, this time setting a kindly seal upon the lock. She was tired. She was content. It had to be faced – Belladonna Agrimony was happy.